www.yessetaddon

Jobbs 'r, Isle of Wight

THIS BOOK BELONGS TO:

www.zoingimage.com

Printed by CreateSpace with chlorine-free ink on
FSC-certified, acid-fee paper which is
30% post-consumer waste recycled material.

No animal by-products or animal-tested ingredients
have been used in the production of this book.

"THE ONLY OBLIGATION WHICH I HAVE A RIGHT TO ASSUME IS TO DO AT ANY TIME THAT WHAT I THINK RIGHT,"

HENRY DAVID THOREAU
(1817–1862 AD)

More Luke Walker: animal stick up for-er

By Violet Plum

with illustrations by Miranda Lemon

Little Chicken Books
Brighton, East Sussex, England
little-chicken.net

More Luke Walker: animal stick up for-er

First published in Great Britain in 2017
By Little Chicken Books
Brighton, East Sussex, England
little-chicken.net

ISBN: 978-1978201729

Many thanks to the creators and distributors of
the fonts used in this book
(most downloaded from fontsquirrel.com):

Kingthings Trypewriter 2 by Kevin King of
kingthingsfonts.co.uk

ZDumb and IMPACT LABEL by Michael Tension of
Tension Type

POILET TAPER and Idolwild by Jakob Fischer of
pizzadude.dk

Disgusting Behavior and AUdimat by Eduardo Recife of
misprintedtype.com

Daniel by Daniel Midgley of
goodreasonblog.blogspot.com

Digory Doodles from fontsquirrel.com

Alex Brush by TypeSETit of typesetit@att.net

Gondola SD Swash by Steve Deffeyes of deffeyes.com

Caprice by George Williams at 1001fonts.com
TOP SECRET by Koczman Bálint
Promocyja public domain font

Please accept my sincere apologies if I've missed
anyone

CONTENTS

And now he's nine ....

Chapter Nine:

Luke Walker and the Secret Society

Luke Walker and the secret society

Luke handed his notebook to Joe.

"Read that and if you agree, write ya name there, under mine, and then put ya thumb print there," he said, pointing to the designated pages.

He uncapped the bottle of black poster paint and squirted a dollop into the saucer while Joe read the pledge.

"D'you agree?" he asked him when he'd finished. Joe nodded. "Are you sure? Do you solemnly swear?"

Luke knew he could not over-emphasize the gravity of this decision. Once you became an outlaw there was no going back.

"I'm sure," said Joe, picking up the Biro and writing his name on the line under Luke's.

Luke was very happy. He ceremoniously pushed the saucer across the carpet to Joe who dipped his thumb into the paint a little too enthusiastically. Thankfully he avoided messing up the book by wiping off the excess on his trousers before pressing his thumb onto the page alongside Luke's handwritten pledge:

SECRET SERSIETY OF ANIMAL STICK UP FOR-ERS

PLEJ:
WE, THE OUTLAWS, PROMISE
  TO HELP THE ANIMALS WHEN
THEY ARE SAD OR FRITENED
  OR HURT.
EVEN IF WE ARE NOT ALOWD
  WE WILL FLY UNDER THE
  RAYDAR.

When Joe passed the book back, Luke forced himself to purse his lips and simulate a frown as he turned to the next page. It was vital that Joe had no illusions about the seriousness of the commitment he had made.

"These are the rules we live by," he said

gravely as he spun the book around and pushed it back to Joe.

SECRET SERSIETY RULES:

ALL MEMBERS ARE OUTLAWS WHO DO NOT LISSEN TO GROWN UPS WHO TELL THEM TO DO SOMETHIN UNKIND (LIKE **EAT YOUR MEAT** OR **WEAR YOUR SHOES MADE OF COW SKIN**)
ALL OUTLAWS ARE LIKE ROBIN HOOD SAVIN THE POOR PEEPUL FROM THE SHERIF OF NOTTINAM, ONY THE POOR PEEPUL ARE THE ANIMALS AND THE SHERIF OF NOTTINAM IS THE PEEPUL WHO WANTS TO EAT THEM OR PUT THEM IN CAGES OR TAKE THEIR BABIES AWAY FROM THEM.
THE OUTLAWS DON'T EAT ANIMALS WICH IS UNKIND AND THEY DON'T EAT THINGS STOLE FROM ANIMALS LIKE EGGS AND MILK AND THEY DON'T WARE THER SKIN.
OUTLAWS ALWAYS REMEMBER THAT ANIMALS HAVE FEELINGS AND THEY WANT TO GO WHERE THEY WANT, LIKE US, AND DO WHAT THEY WANT, LIKE US, AND BE WITH THEIR FAVERITE FRENDS AND RELATIONS, LIKE US, AND NOT BE KILLED OR IN PRISON.

"Do I get one now?" asked Joe when he'd finished reading the rules. Luke thought he was getting ahead of himself.

"Do you agree to the rules?" he asked.

"Yes. I do. That's why I want to be in the club."

"It's not a club, it's a secret ..." he paused suddenly, "shh, someone's out there!" Luke swiftly closed the book and slid it under the bed. He silently got to his feet and crept to the door. He listened. He could hear breathing on the other side. He yanked the door open to reveal his brother, standing frozen stiff with his mouth open.

"Jared! What are you doin'? This is private!"

Jared laughed.

"Nobody cares about your stupid secrets. I'm going to Mike's, Mum told me to tell you it's your turn to do the drying up."

Luke slammed the door and waited until he heard Jared go downstairs.

Joe raised his eyebrows.

Luke Walker and the secret society

"So, do I get one?"

Luke shrugged.

"I s'pose it would be good if you had one, but you'll 'ave to get it yourself. I made this one out of my Maths book. You can use any subject though coz it don't matter what colour it is, as long as it's got plenty of blank pages left. Just tear out the used ones."

Joe nodded.

"But the most important thing you need is a code-maker," Luke went on, "this is mine."

He revealed two circles of cardboard fastened together, that he'd secreted between the pages of his Batman annual.

"Look here," he said, pointing to another page in the notebook, "I've done diagrams to show you how to make one. When you've done it we can send each other coded messages that no one else will be able to decode."

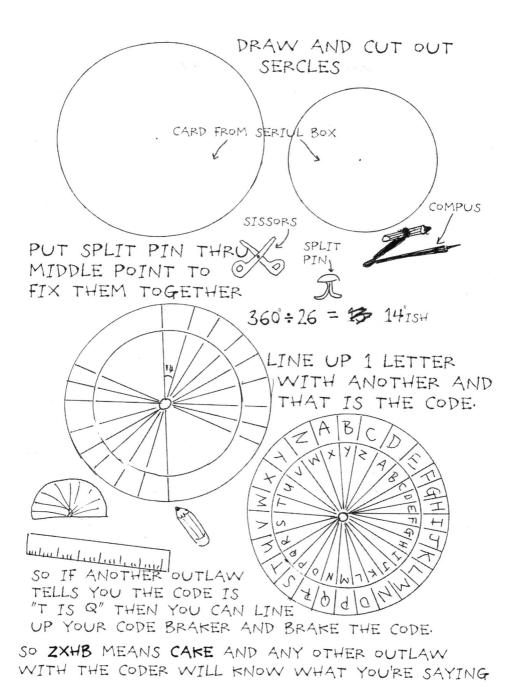

DRAW AND CUT OUT SERCLES

CARD FROM SERIUL BOX

SISSORS

COMPUS

SPLIT PIN

PUT SPLIT PIN THRU MIDDLE POINT TO FIX THEM TOGETHER

$360° ÷ 26 = 14°$ ISH

LINE UP 1 LETTER WITH ANOTHER AND THAT IS THE CODE.

SO IF ANOTHER OUTLAW TELLS YOU THE CODE IS "T IS Q" THEN YOU CAN LINE UP YOUR CODE BRAKER AND BRAKE THE CODE.

SO **ZXHB** MEANS **CAKE** AND ANY OTHER OUTLAW WITH THE CODER WILL KNOW WHAT YOU'RE SAYING

Luke Walker and the secret society

When Joe was clear about how to do it, he went home to make one for himself.

"Don't tell anyone!" Luke reminded him on his way out.

After hearing the front door close, Luke stood at the window and watched Joe walk out of the cul-de-sac feeling full of optimism. Now there were two of them. He'd always known he could rely on Joe, and had benefited from his help a couple of times already, but it was really something to know that his best friend now properly understood that animals needed sticking up for every day; and that sometimes you have to be sneaky about it.

"Luuuke! Come and do the drying up please!" Mum's voice called from downstairs.

"In a minute," he called back. He just needed to wash up the saucer of paint before it dried.

"Now!"

Luke Walker and the secret society

On the other hand, perhaps it was prudent to go down right away.

***

Once the drying up was done, Luke hung out with the damsons in the garden for a while. He gave them yesterday's left over salad, and supervised to make sure Rusty didn't eat it all. She was one naughty rabbit! Ash could look after himself but Scratcher was never quick enough and Rusty would pinch her share given the chance. Luke made them a clean bed, and picked them some raspberries that were too high up on the canes for them to reach before coming back inside to get Dudley for his walk.

"Wear your mac," said Mum, "looks like rain." Luke grabbed his Spiderman cagoule from the hall cupboard and called his dog.

"Dudleeeey. Dudleey. Dudley!" Finally the sleepy boy emerged from Luke's room at the top of the stairs and trotted down, tail wagging.

Luke Walker and the secret society

Was that mud? Luke couldn't think where Dudley could have been to get one of his paws muddy - it hadn't rained yet. But not too worry, it would dust off the carpet when it dried.

Outside it was breezy and the purplish-grey sky looked ominous but Luke and Dudley weren't afraid. They walked briskly to the allotments to see Curly and her beloved lamb, Squirt, and check they had everything they needed. Little Squirt, who wasn't so little any more, came running up to meet them and he and Dudley ambled off to play together. The big allotment plot provided them with plenty of grass and clover to eat but Curly knew Luke was carrying treats and nuzzled against his leg until he gave her the carrots he'd brought. Then he refilled their water trough by stretching the long hose from Dad's plot. In the big shed Luke mucked out the droppings and made a deep, fresh bed of clean hay. Mm, it smelled good. Curly looked in to see what he was up to.

"I just tidied up," Luke told her and he plopped down on the soft hay and rolled around in it. The sound of raindrops on the roof made it extra cosy and Curly decided to join him. She settled herself into a comfortable spot and started chewing - mostly hay but occasionally hair.

"Ow!" Luke yanked his head away and sat up to stroke her. She liked that. Suddenly the rain started coming down hard, sending Dudley and Squirt for cover. They rolled in the hay to dry themselves off, and then the four friends sat together and watched the downpour. The storm was powerful and awe-inspiring. It was exciting to be so close to it.

The rain lasted for almost an hour and when it stopped Luke and Dudley made a break for it. With any luck they would be home before it came down again. That wouldn't keep them dry though. When they reached the village shop a passing lorry relocated a giant puddle at the edge of the road to the exact spot in which Luke and Dudley were standing. Dudley promptly shook. Luke got wetter. Dripping from head to toe, he noticed a card in the shop window. It read:

Baby rabbits
only £5 each
Available from Tues July 2nd
collect from 7 High Street
Call Mindy on 07521333400

"Blimin' breeders!" thought Luke, "them babies'll prob'ly be left in small cages all on their own. An' there's already too many pets who don't get looked after prop'ly! When I'm Prime Minister I'll make it against the law for humans to breed!"

He knew he had to do something but since the shop man suspected him of throwing away five hundred KFC leaflets that Jared was supposed to have delivered on his paper round last week, he needed to keep his head down for the time being. Luckily he belonged to a secret society of animal stick up for-ers so he could delegate. He decided to write a message to Joe. No one would suspect Joe.

As soon as he got home he rushed up to his room and took out his code-maker. After some time he wrote on a scrap of paper:

PWGA NWXXEP YWNZ KBB ODKL SEJZKS

$$T = P$$

When translated it would read:

TAKE RABBIT CARD OFF SHOP WINDOW.

He sealed it in a small brown envelope and wrote on the front

TO JOE CURRANT
PRIVUT

As soon as he'd dropped it through Joe's letter box he was satisfied the job would get done. Joe was the most faithful, dependable person he knew. He needn't give it another thought.

***

Tuesday morning, the first day back to school after teacher-training day, Luke overslept. Teacher-training days always left him muddled as to what day it was and, thinking it was still the weekend, he'd turned over and gone back to sleep after Mum woke him. Dreading the moaning and complaining that were inevitable from Mrs Tebbut, Luke opened the classroom door at twenty two minutes past nine. There was a lot of moaning and complaining going on but none of it directed at him. In fact, no one even noticed him come in. Mrs Tebbut was very agitated, talking to the caretaker at the front of the room.

"It won't come off?" she was very put out.

"I've tried everything," he explained, "hot soapy water with a scouring sponge; vinegar;

lemon juice; bicarbonate of soda; everything I could think of that wouldn't damage the glass."

"So what can I do? I need to be able to see out the back!"

"Maybe you could call a valeting service. They might have special kit that could get it off - maybe a steam cleaner."

Luke slid into his seat next to Joe and quietly asked what was going on. Joe looked worried.

"I got your message," he mumbled, trying to suppress an involuntary smile.

"Oh, good, have you done it?"

"What do you think?"

"I don't know, I didn't pass the shop this morning."

"What are you talkin' about?"

"What are you talkin' about?"

"Your message, I've done it - that's why she's so cross," Joe whispered, trying not to look guilty.

"Why would she be cross about it?" Luke was confused. So was Joe.

"What did you expect? Of course she'd be cross - I used the brown stuff. Why did you want me to do that anyway?"

"What brown stuff? What are you talkin' about?!" Luke's irritation hurt Joe's feelings. He'd successfully completed his first solo mission for the secret society and couldn't understand Luke's reaction. By this time Mrs Tebbut was thanking Mr Pine for trying to help and calling the class to order.

"I did what you asked!" Joe hissed, "I thought you'd be a bit more grateful!" and he passed his translation under the desk to Luke. It read:

tape tebbit ears onn baep window

Chapter Ten:

Luke Walker and the allergic reactions

Luke was hesitant. If he made a mistake now it could cost him the game. Janeway was a good card. She had a lot of Starfleet Authority and was also very cunning. But which to choose, that was the important question.

"Come ohn," said Joe, "it's borin' when you just sit there. Choose one."

"Okay, erm, I choose ..." he hesitated again. He really needed to win this round. He took a deep breath, looked Joe in the eye and said,

"Janeway. Cunning: 45."

Joe looked at his next card and smiled.

"Worf. Cunning: 49."

"Blast! I knew I should have chosen Starfleet Authority! What's Worf's Starfleet Authority?"

"I'm not telling you that!" said Joe, laughingly holding his cards close to his chest.

"Well, it can't be higher than Janeway's. She was Captain. Worf wasn't captain was he?"

Luke Walker and the allergic reactions

Luke consoled himself with the notion that he would have won if Joe hadn't rushed him. If he'd just been able to think about it for a bit longer he would certainly have chosen Starfleet Authority instead of Cunning. Joe really should learn not to rush people, it's not sportsman-like. Luke had one card left. It was Joe's turn to choose the statistic.

"Neelix. To Boldly Go: 20."

"What?!" Luke looked at his card in disbelief. "Neelix can't be better than Spock at boldly goin'!"

He sighed and handed it over.

"Spock. To Boldly Go: 15"

"Yesss! I have triumphed! The cards are mine, all mine, ha ha ha haaa," Joe revelled in his rare victory.

"I'm hungry," said Luke, pretending not to care.

"Me too," his friend agreed and they took

Luke Walker and the allergic reactions

out their lunch boxes. Joe peeked apprehensively between the two slices of Hovis Best of Both which made up his sandwich. Sadly the peanut butter he'd hoped for was not present. Luke was adding crisps to his Marmite and beetroot sandwiches.

"The crunch makes 'em extra good," he explained. Then, "uh oh, has she done it again?"

Joe nodded as he removed two slices of ham and bit into his plain bread and margarine.

"You've got to tell 'er," said Luke, tipping a few of his crisps into Joe's lunch box.

"I have told her, she won't listen!" Joe complained, "I said I'm not eatin' meat or cheese no more and she said, 'course you are!' and that was that! She won't listen. It's okay, I just put it in the bin when she's not lookin'."

"What about your dad - you could tell 'im to explain it to 'er."

"He won't. He just says 'ya mother knows best' and 'listen to ya mother!'. I'll just have to be vegetarian in secret 'til I leave home."

Luke frowned.

"That doesn't sound like a good idea. It'll be pretty borin' jus' livin' on bread an' marg.."

"That's okay," said Joe as he took another bite, "thanks for the crisps," he added.

"That's it! That's what we'll do! Outlaws have to help each other!"

"What?"

"I'll tell my mum I'm more hungry and I need a bigger packed lunch, with an extra sandwich an' an extra bag o'crisps an' an extra cake an' an extra apple ... then I can give half of it to you!"

Joe liked that idea.

"Yeah! Thanks Luke. D'you think she'll do it?"

"No problem," said Luke confidently.

***

Dinner was almost over and Jared was helping Mum clear the table.

"Hurry up Luke," Jared was impatient to get to Youth Club and wasn't allowed to go until he'd done the washing up.

"You want me to get indigestion I suppose!" said Luke, not really surprised that his brother would be so blasé about the dangers of rushing one's food. He'd learned about them from the Rennie advert. "You want me to get acid an' a burnin' heart from eatin' too fast do you?"

Truth be told, Luke was just full up. He really wanted that last roast potato but knew he couldn't swallow another mouthful. He pushed his plate away.

"Go on then - take it," he said, feigning self-sacrifice.

Mum ignored them both and went upstairs to run a bath. Luke followed her.

"Do you want your lavender bubble bath Mum?" he asked helpfully, "the one I got you for your birthday?"

Mrs Walker smiled.

"Yes please, it's on my dressing table."

Luke brought it to her.

"D'you want me to get your KT Tunstall CD? The one I gave you for Mother's Day?"

"Wasn't that from both of you?"

"Yeah, but it was me what chose it. Jared wanted to get you a set of tea towels but I said that wasn't a relaxin' present. I told 'im Mother's Day is for mothers to relax so it had to be a relaxin' present."

Mum nodded slowly.

Luke Walker and the allergic reactions

"Is there something you want Luke?" she asked.

"No, you just have a nice bath. I'll get the CD for you," he volunteered.

"Wait," said Mum, quiet but firm. "What do you want?"

"Oh nothin' really,"

"Luke."

"Well it's nothin' much, jus' thought I'd better mention that I've bin feelin' hungrier at lunch times and I could really do with a bigger lunch."

"Really?" She raised her eyebrows and tilted her head, "since when?"

"Well, jus' this week really, but I think I'll be hungrier from now on coz I'm growin' fast."

"Are you?"

"Yes."

"So, just how much extra food do you think you'll need?"

Luke Walker and the allergic reactions

"Prob'ly about twice as much I should think," he said nonchalantly.

"Twice as much?" she exclaimed with exaggerated surprise, "So that would be two sandwiches, two bags of crisps, four pieces of fruit and two cakes?"

Luke nodded.

Mum shook her head.

"I'm sorry Luke, we just don't have enough money in the budget to give you two lunches every day. I'm sorry if that means you'll stop growing but we should be thankful that you've had a good spurt recently."

Luke had a sneaking suspicion she was being facetious. He frowned. As he turned to leave she called him back.

"Don't forget my CD," she reminded him, smiling, "and tell Jared not to give the potato you didn't have room for to Dudley or he'll get the runs."

Luke Walker and the allergic reactions

***

The following morning Joe called for Luke and they walked to school together. When they reached the bins outside the Memorial Hall, Joe stopped and took out his sandwich. Egg mayonnaise. Before Luke could stop him he tossed the whole thing into the bin.

"So, what have we got for lunch today?" Joe smiled, enjoying the quiet rebellion. Luke felt awkward.

"Well, erm, ..."

Joe's smile faded.

"Couldn't you get it?" he asked, disappointed.

"Well, it's not that I couldn't get it," Luke didn't want to admit defeat, "it's just that I was thinkin' a lot about it and I decided that actchally it's not a good idea."

"Why not?" said Joe, feeling hungry already.

"Well, if your mum still gives you meat and

eggs and cheese and stuff, even though you don't eat it, then it's still bein' bought for you, which means animals are still bein' killed for you."

"Oh. Yeah," Joe agreed. He didn't want that.

"So we've got to find a way to make your mum listen," said Luke decisively.

Joe was not hopeful.

"She won't listen."

"She hasn't listened yet," Luke corrected him. He liked a challenge. "We've just got to tell 'er in a way she can't ignore."

Joe sighed. He preferred to do things quietly. Secretly.

"But what will I eat today?" he asked, disheartened.

Luke was busy thinking.

"What? Oh, you can share mine," he said generously, and they continued on to school.

As luck would have it they wouldn't be

Luke Walker and the allergic reactions

short of food that day because class 4 was having a cookery lesson and that meant they'd all brought ingredients with them. They were making scones. Mrs Tebbut never allowed the boys to work together on these things and insisted on choosing their partners for them. As a result, Luke found himself sharing a table with Penelope Bittern. Penelope was very particular about doing things properly.

"Don't put any of your stuff on my half of the table," she instructed, "I can't let it contaminate my stuff."

Luke was affronted.

"There's nothing wrong with my stuff," he told her, "it's clean. It's new packets - haven't even bin opened - look!"

She lifted her arm to shield her side of the table from the sealed bag of flour he thrust towards her.

"You can't put that near my stuff!" she

sounded panicked. "I might be allergic!"

"Allergic to what?"

"I'm allergic to raisins and kiwi fruit so ..."

"I 'aven't got no raisins or kiwis!"

"Sooo, my mum said we're playing it safe 'til they know for sure what else I'm allergic to. I'm having tests."

"Well, you've got the same stuff as me," Luke couldn't abide hypochondriac drama queens, "flour, sugar, margarine - so if you're allergic to mine you're allergic to yours."

"But my ingredients have been specially kept separate from things that might give me allergies - like milk, eggs, peanuts - and ..."

"You can be allergic to milk?"

"Yes, lots of people are, which is why..."

"And what happens to you if you eat it, if you're allergic?"

"Well, that depends," she was gratified he was finally listening to her. "I think it's different

Luke Walker and the allergic reactions

for different people. It depends how serious their allergy is."

"It can be serious?"

"Yes. Some people die if they eat something they're allergic to. Even just a tiny bit of it. Even if it's so tiny you can't hardly see it."

"Okay, now I know you're makin' it up. No one's dyin' from a tiny bit of peanut! You're just a 'ttention seekin' hypochondrian who's makin' stuff up to get the whole table to 'erself!"

That was disappointing. Luke went mentally back to the drawing board.

But Penelope wasn't finished.

"They do! Their throat swells up so they can't breathe! My mum told me and I think she should know 'cause her brother's allergic to nuts and he has to carry a life-saver injection with him all the time in case he accidentally eats one."

"Really?" That sounded real. Penelope

didn't have enough imagination to make up something as cool as that. "What other things might happen to someone who ate somethin' they were allergic to?"

Penelope patiently answered Luke's endless questions and he, in return, took great care to keep his ingredients away from her half of the table. By the end of the lesson Luke knew how to make Joe's mum listen. The hard part, however, would be persuading Joe to do it.

***

Joe swallowed his last bite of overdone scone and made a face that suggested he wasn't enjoying it.

"Not good?" asked Luke. His had been delicious.

"What? Oh, yeah, the scone's good, it's your idea I don't like."

"Drastic times, drastic scissors," Luke reminded him, "I know it's not very nice but it'll be worth it won't it? You need to make it look real or it won't work."

Joe was still reluctant.

"But I don't see why I can't just do the lentil hotpot thing. I could do that. And the not breathin' thing - I can hold my breath longer 'n most people."

"You have to show you're allergic to all three things - milk, eggs and meat - so you have to have three different allergic reactions to be convincin'. Jus' think yourself lucky you've never liked fish, otherwise we'd have to come up with four reactions."

Joe nodded and took the bag Luke handed him. Luke patted him on the back. It was important to give moral support to your soldiers.

"You can do it," he said encouragingly.

Joe walked home from Luke's house, dreading what he had to do, but determined to

Luke Walker and the allergic reactions

do it. Luke was right. It would be worth it.

***

For dinner his mum had cooked lamb chops. After getting to know Curly and Squirt, Joe couldn't bring himself to actually bite into one but when no one was looking he cut a piece off and hid it in his pocket. Then he shoved some mashed potato in his mouth. After swallowing, he started making retching noises.

"Joe! Do you have to make that revolting noise?" his mum asked with disgust, "what's the matter?"

Joe jumped up from the table and ran to the toilet. Mrs Currant was close behind so he had to be quick. He tipped the pre-opened tin of lentil hotpot, that he'd hidden behind the toilet, into the bowl and then leaned over it and made vomiting noises. Mrs Currant caught up.

"Oh, Joe, have you got a stomach bug? I hope the rest of us don't catch it!"

Luke Walker and the allergic reactions

Joe looked up at her.

"No," he said pathetically, "I think I'm allergic to meat." He bit his lip as he remembered Luke had told him not to tell her he was allergic, but to let her work it out for herself.

Mrs Currant looked in the toilet, saw the orange slop and thought with revulsion how different a person's food looked when it came back up from how it looked when it went down, only moments before. She looked at her son, he did look pale.

"Okay, you go and lay down. I'll bring you a glass of water and a bucket."

Luke Walker and the allergic reactions

"So far so good," thought Joe and went to bed, hungry.

In the morning, he was even hungrier but knew he had to ditch one more meal. As it was Saturday, breakfast consisted not only of cereal, but also fried eggs on toast. First the cereal - Joe tipped the choco pops into his bowl and covered them with cows' milk. He put a spoonful into his mouth and immediately spat it back and grabbed his throat. He gasped.

"I can't breathe!" he whispered desperately as he bent his head to his knees and reached in his pyjama pocket for Luke's mum's blue eyeshadow. He rubbed his fingertip into the colour and smeared it across his lips before lifting up his head to reveal it to .... no one. The room was empty. His dad had taken his plate into the living room to watch the news and his mum had gone to get the paper from the front door. Joe continued to hold his breath, hoping his mum would return before he was forced to exhale. Just then the kitchen door opened and his older sister, Janet, walked in.

"That better not be my eyeshadow," she warned him.

"It's not," he assured her, forgetting not to breathe just as Mrs Currant re-entered the kitchen.

"Mum, Joe's messing up my eyeshadow."

Mrs Currant looked at Joe then screwed up her face and shook her head.

"That's not yours. Yours is more turquoise," she said and sat at the table to read the paper.

Part two was a bust. Joe loaded his plate with eggs from the pan and toast from the rack before stealing himself to proceed with part three of the plan. He sat down and reached into his other pyjama pocket to get the stinging nettles hidden there. While his mum read her horoscope and Janet searched the fridge for jam, Joe quickly and bravely rubbed the nettles on his forearms and neck before hiding them again in his pocket. The pain was immediate. It stung a lot.

He chopped and mashed one of his eggs with his fork to make it look as if he'd eaten some of it. Then, as he noticed the white bumps starting to appear on his arms he said,

"Mum! Mum!" and rubbed his arms and neck furiously with the palms of both hands.

Mother and daughter both looked at him.

"How on earth did you get stung in here?" Janet said in high-pitched disbelief.

"I didn't," Joe argued, in genuine distress, "I'm allergic to eggs!"

"Stop rubbing it like that, silly boy!" Mrs Currant grabbed a tea towel from the drawer and ran it under the cold tap. "Here,

Luke Walker and the allergic reactions

put this over the bumps, keep them cool 'til they go down. And maybe have a look in the garden for a dock leaf to rub on it."

"It's not stingers," Joe protested, "I'm allergic to eggs!"

"Honestly Joe," said his mum, shaking her head and returning to the horoscopes, "only you could get stung at the breakfast table."

"Boys," said Janet derisively.

Joe had had enough. His skin was burning and itching and stinging - he was in real pain and they still didn't listen.

"I'M A VEGETARIAN!" he shouted.

"Joseph Currant! How dare you raise your voice to me?!" said Mrs Currant, shocked by his impertinence.

"Keep the noise down in there! I'm trying to watch the news!" Mr Currant yelled from the living room.

"And now you've upset your father," his

Luke Walker and the allergic reactions

mother went on.

Joe looked at his hands.

"I don't want to eat meat no more," he said quietly, "or eggs or fish or milk, or cheese," he finished, getting quieter with every word.

"Oh, I get it," Joe's mum said, knowingly, "you want to be like your little friend don't you?" she peered at him over the newspaper. "You don't have to copy everything he does you know."

"No, that's not ..." Joe tried to explain.

"I know what it's like, it's not that long since I was at school myself you know. Of course I was vegetarian, long before it was fashionable," she boasted.

"Why'd you stop then?" Joe wondered.

"But then I married your father and you can't imagine him giving up his sausages and his bacon can you? Ha! I'd like to see the woman who could pull that off!"

"Mm," said Joe.

Luke Walker and the allergic reactions

"Talking of which, I bet you haven't thought this through, - if you do this you won't be able to have fish fingers any more."

"I never eat fish fingers. I don't like ..."

"And no more ice cream, or cake,"

"You can get special ice cream and ..."

"Oh my boy, you don't know what you're letting yourself in for!"

Joe looked at her, holding his breath.

"I know what you're letting yourself in for - been there, done that!"

She studied him through squinting eyes. Joe said nothing. She seemed to be considering it. After a couple of minutes she made a decision.

"Well, alright. But I'm not making special meals just for you. You can have whatever we're having with some extra vegetables instead of the meat. Is that acceptable Your Highness?"

Joe looked up and smiled.

"Yes," he said, "thank you."

His mum returned the smile and ruffled his hair.

"Boys," she said, slowly shaking her head.

Joe pressed the damp tea towel against his throbbing skin and smiled. Janet scrunched up her nose and stuck out her tongue at him.

"I give it a month!" she whispered.

Joe just carried on smiling.

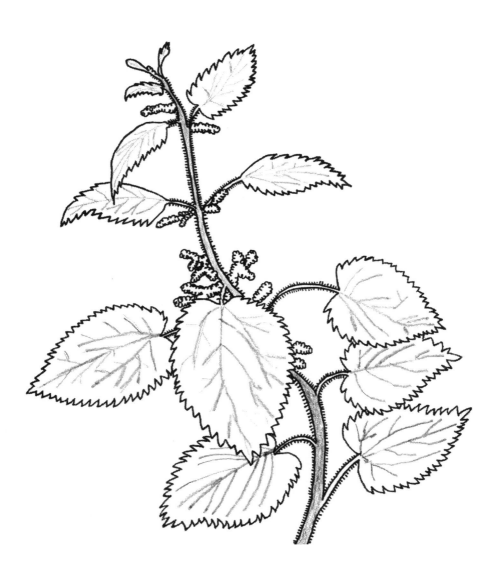

Luke Walker and the allergic reactions

Chapter Eleven:

Luke Walker and the ice cream van

Luke Walker and the ice cream van

Set apart from the rest of the flea market was a stall that was of great interest to Luke. Standing behind it was a lady wearing black eye shadow and black nail varnish. She had long, straight, jet black hair and her khaki jacket had lots of badges on it which said things like "MEAT IS MURDER" and "A FISH IS NOT A VEGETABLE" and "NOT YOUR MUM" written above a picture of a man suckling from a cow.

"Where'd you get those?" Luke asked the lady.

"These? Oh, different places. This one I ordered from a website," she said, indicating the one with the suckling business man, "and these I got from Vegfest."

"What's Vegfest?"

"It's a weekend event with lots of stalls and talks by veggies and veggie companies. They have them a couple of times a year in different cities like London and Brighton."

Luke Walker and the ice cream van

Luke had never met another vegetarian before, apart from Joe, and he'd had no idea there were enough of them to warrant weekend events like that. He was impressed.

"Are you interested in becoming vegan?" the lady asked as Luke browsed the leaflets on display.

"Vegan?" said Luke, "That's not a real word! I'm a veggietareun and I wun't be nothin' else!"

"Well that's good, but why are you a vegetarian? Is it because you don't want animals to be killed?"

"Of course," said Luke.

"Well then, it might interest you to know that animals are also killed to supply you with milk and eggs," the lady explained, with patience.

"I know that, that's why I don't eat 'em because I'm a veggie-tareun!" said Luke, slowly, with emphasis. Not patience. "Veggie (that's short for vegetables) tareun (that means someone what eats 'em). I on'y eat vegetables, which means things what grow after bein' planted in the ground." It must be acknowledged that Luke was good at explaining things.

The lady looked as though she now understood and was very pleased about it.

"That means you're a vegan young man, well done!"

Luke was unswayed.

"I'll stick with words what make sense, thanks."

The stall-holder smiled again. The word didn't matter. Then she realised the boy had been browsing for a good few minutes and no responsible adult had materialised.

"Who did you come here with?" she asked, "is your mum or dad or somebody around here somewhere?"

Luke nodded.

"Mmm, somewhere."

Luke Walker and the ice cream van

He continued browsing. There was a lot of interesting stuff. People needed to know this stuff.

"Where do you get these leaflets from?" he asked the lady.

"Why? Do you want some? You can take what you want," she replied generously.

Luke couldn't believe his luck.

"Just take 'em? As many as I want?"

"Yes," the lady assured him, "they need to get out to the public; people need to know this stuff."

"Yes they do!" said Luke, gratified to have found a kindred spirit, "have you got a box?"

"You want that many?" the lady raised her eyebrows, "it'll be quite heavy if you fill a box. How will you carry it? How will you get it home?"

"I've got a wheelbarra," said Luke, proudly pointing to a rusty old one he'd bought for 50p ten minutes earlier, "an' I'm not takin' 'em home."

Luke Walker and the ice cream van

He smiled broadly as he considered how fortuitous this outing had turned out to be; how lucky it was that this week of all weeks he'd needed a wheelbarrow.

***

Nan and Grandad loved to go to car boot sales, antique fairs and flea markets. They would drive for miles to get to them and rarely a Sunday went by without Nan acquiring a 'new' old plant pot, or handbag, or garden bench, or record or book or who knows what. So, when Luke decided he needed a few tools for his allotment - a rake, a bucket or two, and a wheelbarrow - he asked Mum to ask Nan if he could go with them that weekend. She said yes, as long as he behaved himself and didn't eat or drink anything in Grandad's car, or put his feet on the seats.

"Will she ever get over the chocolate biscuit/chewing gum incident?" he thought. "It wasn't even my gum - it had got stuck on my shoe because of a dropper and the chocolate crumbs ... "

Anyway, he promised to be good, and it was arranged.

Six days later, Luke was sitting in the back of Grandad's car; seatbelt on; feet on the floor; no food or drink whatsoever. They turned into a farm lane and drove past a field of grazing cows, one of whom had a baby with her. They waited in a long queue of cars

Luke Walker and the ice cream van

approaching the flea market and Luke was able
to watch mother and baby for a few minutes.
He could see how attentive the mother was to
her baby and how the baby followed his mother
wherever she went. It was nice to watch.
Then he saw two farmers with a wheelbarrow
walk over to them and lift the baby into it.
The baby cried out for his mum and the mum
tried to get to her baby but one of the
farmers obstructed her so that the other one
could wheel the barrow away. He walked briskly,
almost breaking into a run to get to the gate
as quickly as possible and the mother cow
hurried after them, calling all the time to her
baby and him calling back to her. The farmer
with the wheelbarrow got through the gate and
closed it and the other one climbed the fence.
They put the calf into a trailer and drove away
in the Land Rover that towed it, along the
track that bordered the field, until they got

Luke Walker and the ice cream van

to the road and were soon out of sight. The whole time the mother cow was running along the edge of the field, trying to keep up with them, calling for her baby. When the trailer was out of sight she just stood at the fence and called and called, a most miserable, pining sound, as she watched the direction in which they'd fled, pleading for her baby's return.

"Where are they takin' 'im? Are they gonna bring 'im back?" Luke desperately asked his grandparents.

"What love?" said Nan. She hadn't been watching.

"The baby cow! They took 'im away from 'is mum! Why did they do that? When will they bring 'im back?"

"They won't," said Grandad, matter-of-factly.

"What?! Why not?" Luke demanded.

"The farmer keeps cows for their milk. He

needs to sell as much milk as possible so he can't have the calves drinking his profits can he? He's got to make a living. Way of the world Luke, you might as well get used to it."

Luke was outraged. He'd known instinctively that it wasn't right to steal a cow's milk and was certain it couldn't be natural to drink it if you weren't a baby cow, but he'd had no idea that farmers actually kidnapped babies away from their mothers; that a mother who'd done nothing wrong, who was giving him her milk, was not even allowed to keep the baby who made the milk possible. And the baby - what would happen to the baby?

"Does everybody know this? Does everybody know what the horrible farmer is doin'?" Luke felt that surely people wouldn't buy the milk if they knew.

"He's not horrible Luke," Nan tried to explain, "cows are not people, they don't have the same

Luke Walker and the ice cream van

feelings and emotional attachments that we have."

"Yes they do! Din't you see? Din't you see 'em together? They love each other!"

"Luke," Nan answered quietly, "the farmer's got to earn ..."

"I could earn a livin' stealin' other people's jewel'ry and sellin' it to someone else, but if I did that you'd tell me off!"

"It's not the same ..."

"Too right it's not the same coz I wun't be kidnappin' someone's baby!"

While Luke fumed Grandad reached the car park and they all got out of the car. Luke couldn't stop thinking about the cow baby and the cow mum crying for each other. He trailed slowly behind his grandparents, very unhappy in the realisation that this was the way of the world and there was nothing he could do about it, not really, not for that baby or that mum.

Luke Walker and the ice cream van

"Grown ups always say 'you must be good', 'you must be kind' and then they do things what they know is unkind," Luke mumbled frustratedly to himself, "they don't follow their own rules, so they can't expect me to follow 'em. They should follow my rules - mine make more sense, mine do what they say instead of just say and not do!"

And so, as he railed against the world, he wandered away from his grandparents and browsed the stalls alone. He wasn't worried. He'd find them later.

***

With a wheelbarrow full of three different leaflets which told the truth about the dairy industry, Luke headed for the car park. The wheelbarrow was heavy and the cars were parked quite close together on uneven ground, so it was rather difficult to stop the barrow from tipping. But Luke was strong and

Luke Walker and the ice cream van

determined so he only lost control of it a couple of times, and on those occasions the cars he grazed were already scratched anyway. He put one leaflet under a wiper blade, on the windscreen of each car. He'd seen it done before with car-wash flyers in the supermarket car park.

Some wipers were easy to lift, some of them required a bit of force, a couple of them came off, but when that happened he was luckily able to find a window or a sunroof open so he tossed the leaflet inside. Considerate as always, he tossed the wiper blade in with it.

Luke Walker and the ice cream van

After some time - he had no idea how much - Luke had leafleted most of the cars in the car park. He had intended not to miss a single one but when he saw an angry man, waving a wiper blade, fast approaching his position, he decided that discretion was the better part of valour and retreated behind the long queues for the portaloos. He had almost half a box of leaflets left and wanted to use them. It wasn't long before he found an opportunity.

The ice cream van was parked close to the line of trees which skirted the market. It was doing a roaring trade. Luke felt that it wouldn't do any trade at all if there was any justice in the world. He was sure it wouldn't if everyone knew the truth. That thought gave him an idea. This idea, he was well aware, was not, strictly speaking, legal. But it was moral and that meant he was right to do it. He would do what Robin Hood would have done,

Luke Walker and the ice cream van

whatever the consequences. He was an outlaw after all.

He left his wheelbarrow in the shadows behind the trees and ran back to a craft stall he'd seen earlier. The lady on the craft stall was demonstrating how to make paper maché models. She was doing the 'here's one I made earlier' bit, revealing a stiff, hollow, paper pig ready for a coat of paint. The tub of wallpaper paste that she'd been using in an earlier part of her demonstration was tucked away under her stall.

"I jus' need to borra a bit," Luke told himself, "I'll bring it back before she misses it."

Within minutes he was pasting leaflets all over one side of the ice cream van, unseen by the ice cream seller or his treat-seeking customers who stood in line on the other side. He worked fast, knowing he might be spotted and stopped at any moment. At the same time he was encouraged by a feeling that some great spirit was watching over him, enabling him to complete his mission unhindered. The spirit of Robin Hood? It couldn't just have been luck that he'd been able to get his hands on exactly what he needed for this job. The label on the side of the tub of paste read:

MELROSE WHEATPASTE
suitable for paper maché, scrapbooking
wallpaper application & billboard posters
NON TOXIC * STRONG * DRIES TRANSPARENT
WARNING: WHEATPASTE POSTERS, ONCE APPLIED, ARE DIFFICULT TO REMOVE.

Luke Walker and the ice cream van

It couldn't have been more perfect. Luke fearlessly pasted over colourful illustrations of lollipops, ice cream cones, and a happy cartoon cow who bore no resemblance to her real-life counterparts. The van's lies were soon obliterated by pages of facts and figures about the cruel reality of dairy farming, including miserable photographic proof. When the side of the van was completely covered in leaflets, as high as Luke could reach, he stepped back to see the full effect. It was good.

Unable to believe how well this was going, Luke slipped unseen, back the way he'd come. He re-emerged from behind the line of trees when he reached the craft stall and returned the paste. Then he tucked the remaining four leaflets in his back pocket and pushed his empty wheelbarrow from stall to stall, looking for Nan and Grandad. He looked for ages until eventually he came close to the organisers' table and heard his own name over the Tannoy.

"Would Luke Walker please go to the ice cream van. Would Luke Walker please go to the ice cream van, near the car park and the toilets."

Luke stood still, his face flushed hot.

"They know!" he thought with horror.

It got worse. He watched as two police officers walked up to the organisers' table. After a few moments a man there pointed in Luke's direction. The police officers started to walk towards him. He ran. All he could think was that he needed to get out of there. They might know his name but would they know his address? He didn't look behind, that would be suspicious, he just ran as fast as he could. The wheelbarrow was slowing him down. He had to leave it.

He climbed the low post and rail fence and

Luke Walker and the ice cream van

jumped down into the car park. His first instinct was to find Grandad's car, but then he thought that if they knew his name, they might know who his grandparents were, they might be waiting for him there. He hesitated, crouched between a Mini and a Fiesta, and tried to see Grandad's car without being seen. Yes, that was it, and there was Grandad. With another policeman.

There was nothing for it, he had to go back into the market, he had to try to be invisible in the crowd. But he was scared and wanted an ally. He made a beeline for the black-haired lady's stall.

The lady, who was just beginning to pack up her stall, putting leaflets back in their boxes, was surprised to see Luke racing towards her, all red in the face and out of breath, looking like he feared for his life.

"Hide me!" said Luke desperately, and sunk to

Luke Walker and the ice cream van

the floor behind the biggest box.

The lady was alarmed.

"What's wrong? What are you ...?"

"Shhh!" said Luke in a vehement whisper, "don't talk to me! Don't look at me! They might be watching!"

"But ..."

"Excuse me Miss," another woman's voice interrupted her. She turned to face a police-woman.

"Is this your stall?" she asked.

"Yes it is."

"And your name is?"

"Jessica Rabbit. Would you like a leaflet?"

"I would like to have a look, yes, thank you," and the policewoman began to paw the various piles. "Is this all you've got?"

The black-haired lady casually dropped her jacket on top of Luke as another officer stepped around the stall to look in the boxes.

"I've got these as well," she answered, "as you can see," and she lifted the boxes onto the table so that they wouldn't need to rummage around the other side.

The policewoman found what she was looking for - three different anti-dairy leaflets.

"Is there any reason you were hiding these?" she asked.

The lady laughed.

"I wasn't hiding them, I was just in the process of packing up," she explained.

The police officers exchanged cynical glances and while the male picked up the box of leaflets, the female addressed the stall-holder.

"I am arresting you on suspicion of offences under section 1 of the Criminal Damage Act 1971. You do not have to say anything, but it may harm your defence if you do not mention when questioned something you later rely on in court. Anything you do say may be given in evidence. Do you understand?"

"Not remotely," the lady replied, "what am I supposed to have done?"

Luke stayed motionless under the lady's jacket. He felt bad that she was getting blamed for what he'd done, but was somehow unable to move or speak. He just sat still until he couldn't hear them any more. He waited till they'd gone.

When he stood up and watched them retreat past the other stalls, seemingly diminished in size, his courage returned. He donned the khaki jacket, pulled the hood over his head and cautiously followed. The officers and their captive approached a police car and the policewoman opened a rear door, put her hand on the black-haired lady's head and assisted her into the back seat.

Luke was worried they would drive away before he could get to them but luck was on his side again. Another policeman with a camera called to his colleagues and they walked a few steps away from the car to talk to him. That was Luke's chance.

The police car was between him and the officers so he kept his head down and crept up to the rear door. He tried the handle. Nothing happened. He tried it again. It should have opened. He'd seen Dad do it a hundred times. A car's back doors were only locked on the inside. The black-haired lady looked out the window, shook her head and spoke almost inaudibly.

"What are you doing? Go away! Quickly! Before they see you!"

Luke didn't listen. He was determined to rescue her. This lady was a righteous warrior like himself; a fighter for justice; a fellow animal stick up for-er. He would rescue her or die in the attempt. He tried the door again. It clicked open. It was like dad's car!

Luke Walker and the ice cream van

At that moment the ice cream van pulled up between the police car and the police officers, thus enlightening the black-haired lady on the reason for her arrest. The ice cream seller leaned out his window to talk to the officers.

"Get out! Quick!" Luke urged the lady.

The two of them ran as fast as they could back into the market and out the other side towards the trees. When they reached cover they slumped down behind the trees and caught their breath.

"I'm sorry I got you in trouble Jessica," said Luke. The lady grinned.

"What's your name?" she asked.

"Luke."

"Not Luke Walker by any chance?"

"Yeah, how'd you know?"

"They've been calling your name on the Tannoy for the last hour and a half."

"Oh yeah, that's why I had to hide."

Luke Walker and the ice cream van

The lady laughed.

"Oh, it all makes sense now. It wasn't the police, it was your family trying to find you."

Realisation flickered across Luke's features.

"Oh," he said, feeling a little guilty for forgetting about Nan and Grandad. "I'm sorry I got you in trouble," he apologised again.

"Hey, listen, getting blamed for what you did won't do my reputation any harm at all," the lady said with a chuckle. Luke smiled.

"Anyway," she went on, "I'm free and clear now. Thanks for rescuing me."

Luke looked at the lady and thought she could be trusted.

"Would you like to join my secret society?" he asked.

"I like the sound of that! Especially if this is the kind of stuff your secret society gets up to!"

Luke Walker and the ice cream van

"Good," said Luke, "there's on'y me an' Joe so far but that's good coz no one else knows about it. So don't tell anyone."

"I won't," the lady agreed.

"Nobody."

"I won't," she laughingly assured him.

"How will I get in touch with you?" Luke asked.

The lady took a pen out of her pocket and wrote a phone number on the back of Luke's hand.

"Any time, day or night, you can reach me on that number," she said, standing up, "and my name's Kris." She smiled at his mild confusion. "I'd better get out of here before they start searching the woods. Will you be alright? Will you be able to find your people?"

"Yeah."

"Go to the organisers' table, they'll be able to get hold of them for you."

Luke Walker and the ice cream van

Luke wasn't sure.

"Don't worry, the police aren't looking for you. It's safe. Go and find your people," she urged him and then she started away, going deeper into the trees.

"Oh, don't forget your jacket," Luke called after her.

"Keep it," she said, smiling, and left.

Luke walked back through the market to the organisers' table and informed them that he was Luke Walker. Nan's mobile was called and she and Grandad were there to fetch him in next to no time. Nan ran at him, hugged him and then smacked his bum.

"You horrible boy! Why would you do this to us? We've been worried sick! Where have you been?"

"I'm sorry," he said sincerely, "I was jus' shoppin' and I lost track of time."

"Shopping! You weren't supposed to go off

by yourself! You were supposed to stay with us! You knew th..."

"What did you buy?" Grandad interrupted.

Luke looked at him and thought for a moment.

"A wheelbarra ..." he said, turning full circle to look for it. And there it was, lying on its side, just a few metres away. "This one," he added, going to fetch it.

"And a jacket by the look of it," said Nan, a little calmer now.

"Oh yeah," Luke smiled, "and a jacket."

Luke Walker and the ice cream van

Chapter 12:

Luke Walker and the new teacher

Luke Walker and the new teacher

"Search everyone's quarters on decks five to seven."

"It's nillogical to search deck six ..."

"No, you don't say that."

"Why not?"

"Coz you're Tom Paris."

"Paris knows when things aren't logical."

"No he doesn't. Paris don't think like that."

"But ..."

"I'm Tuvok, you're Paris," Luke put his foot down, "say somethin' like 'no don't search deck six coz it smells in there'."

Joe shrugged.

"No, don't search deck six, it smells in there coz that's where Tuvok's quarters is."

"This is a serious situation Mr Paris! My quarters do not smell and even if they did it is nillogical to leave an entire deck out of the search. Search all quarters on decks five, six and seven. Now!"

Luke Walker and the new teacher

"Luke, come downstairs please," Mum called, "I want you to try on your new school uniform."

Luke pulled a face. They would be back at school in three days and he had been trying not to think about it.

"Luuuke, now please."

He reluctantly put down his tricorder and did as he was told. In the living room Mum had all his new clothes laid out on the settee. They looked horrible. Two pairs of grey trousers with a smart crease pressed down the front; four white shirts folded and pinned with cardboard under the collars; five pairs of grey socks; one black sweatshirt with the name of his school written in gold across the front; one black jumper, and new shoes. Luke looked suspiciously at the shoes.

"Are they leather? I'm not wearin' cow skin," he insisted.

"I know they look like it but they're not,"

Mum assured him, "look."

She showed him the label inside and Luke was satisfied that they were made of synthetic materials.

"If they can make shoes what look like leather and feel like leather and do the same job as leather without bein' leather, why do they keep killin' cows?"

"Beats me," said Mum, she really didn't have time to get into it right now. "Okay, try these on. If they don't fit I'll have to take them straight back and change them."

Luke tried it all on and everything fitted perfectly. Mum had a knack for choosing the right size which she was very glad about because it meant she didn't have to take him with her when she went shopping.

"Oh, you do look smart," she said proudly.

Luke scowled.

"I don't like this," he said, pulling at the

black jumper, "it's itchy. What's it made of?"

"Wool."

"Sheep's wool?"

"Lamb's wool act..., oh Luke, don't start. Taking the wool doesn't hurt the lamb, they have to have it sheared so they don't get too hot. It's just like when you have your hair cut. That doesn't hurt does it?"

"How do you know? Have you ever seen a sheep bein' sheared? Or a lamb? I don't think Squirt would like it."

PURE NEW WOOL

Mum looked at the ceiling and took a deep breath.

"Luke, you need a warm jumper for school. Honestly, it doesn't hurt them to have their hair cut."

Luke didn't know what to think. He supposed there could be no harm if the sheep did need to have their wool cut off; if they didn't want it themselves. He decided to let it go for now, but he would have to find out more about it before making a final decision. He tossed the jumper onto the settee and ran back upstairs. He wanted Joe's opinion.

Joe wasn't sure.

"When Janet doesn't know somethin' she looks it up on the computer," he said, "p'rhaps we should do that."

"I bro..., erm, Dad's computer doesn't work anymore and Jared won't let me use his. Can we borra Janet's?"

Joe laughed and shook his head. Luke was stumped.

Luke Walker and the new teacher

"We'll 'ave to investigate it ourselves," he said eventually, "I'm not wearin' that jumper 'til I know for sure it's not hurtin' anybody."

***

Tuesday came around as it was bound to, and Luke found himself back at school. He was predictably annoyed about it but took solace in the fact that at least he wasn't in Mrs Tebbut's class anymore. Everyone knew Ms Robinson was the nicest teacher in school. She never sent anyone to the headmaster or made anyone stand in the corner or made anyone do extra homework when they had trouble doing the normal amount of homework. From what he'd heard, Luke felt sure she was the type of teacher who would sympathise with someone if they accidentally stapled their own finger. And she certainly wasn't the type of teacher to make someone eat all their mushy peas just because they'd asked for a big portion when they couldn't possibly have known they would be so salty.

At ten to nine he and the rest of class 5 were allowed to enter the classroom. There were a lot of unfamiliar faces and not enough desks or seats for everyone. Those who could found seats, others sat on the desks while some, mostly the children Luke had never seen before, just stood around in huddles.

"I know there's not enough seats," said Thomas, Ms Robinson's teaching assistant, "but bear with us. Ms Robinson and Mr Beardsley will be here in a minute and they'll explain everything."

"Who's Mr Beardsley?" asked Katia.

"Ah, here he is. Mr Beardsley, meet Year 5."

At that moment a tall, thin man with very short, sandy hair and glasses walked into the room. He wore a beige knitted waistcoat buttoned up over a white and beige checked shirt. Luke was a little concerned.

Luke Walker and the new teacher

"Good morning everyone," said the man, "I'm Mr Beardsley and I'll be teaching some of you this year."

"Where's Muz Robinson?" shouted Kenny.

"She's still talking to the Headmaster, she'll be here in a moment."

Luke and Joe stood against the back wall feeling rather uneasy. The room hummed with muffled mutterings. Nobody knew what was going on. A few minutes later Ms Robinson joined them.

"Sorry to keep you waiting class 5," she said, "it's all a bit last minute so I hope you'll bear with us."

"If they told us what needs bearin' with, we might be able to," whispered Luke.

Joe nodded. Ms Robinson explained.

"Little Greatoak Primary school has closed due to insufficient attendance. That is, the council has decided it's too expensive to run a whole school when there are not enough pupils to fill it."

Everyone was listening.

"So, all the children from Little Greatoak will be coming to school here from now on." She looked around at the new faces. "Welcome to Gingham County Primary, we hope you'll be very happy here."

Luke, without understanding why, felt suddenly possessive of the school he'd never liked.

"Most classes have had the addition of three or four pupils," Ms Robinson went on, "but Year 5 has been increased by twenty, making a class of fifty pupils which is far too many."

Luke didn't like the way this was going.

"So we're going to have two Year 5 classes: Class 5A and Class 5B. I will take Class 5B and Mr Beardsley - who has also joined us from Little Greatoak - will take Class 5A."

Luke Walker and the new teacher

It could not truthfully be said that Luke was good at maths but even he was quick to work out that, since half of fifty was twenty five, at least some of his old class would not be in Ms Robinson's group. Without realising it, he held his breath.

Mr Beardsley and Ms Robinson stood at the front of the class with open registers in their hands. Ms Robinson continued.

"Class 5B," she said, "we will be moving to the new mobile classroom next to the playground. When I call your name, collect your bags and coats and wait for me in the cloakroom."

Ms Robinson called the names on her register and, one by one, children left the room. Luke realised with horror that the division had been done alphabetically. Ms Robinson was taking the top of the alphabet. Those at the bottom were being left with Mr Beardsley. Joe

Currant's name was called. Luke Walker's was not.

***

At the end of the day Luke couldn't find Joe so he walked home alone feeling very sorry for himself. Then he saw something which took his mind off it. Across the road sheep were being rounded up with two dogs and a quad bike. They looked scared and tried to run in all directions but the dogs and the motorbike kept heading them off so that in the end they had no choice but to enter a fenced paddock at the edge of the field. Unlike the grassy field, this paddock was nothing but mud. There was nothing to eat and nothing to drink. Luke watched from the bus shelter as the quad bike rider locked the gate, ordered the dogs onto the back of the bike, and then rode away. When they were out of sight Luke went over to the sheep. There were thirty or forty of them who recoiled as he approached. Luke wanted to release them but wondered if he should. He couldn't understand why the farmer would lock them in there like that without even a water trough, but maybe the sheep needed some medicine that had to be taken on an empty stomach. It would be wrong to act without knowing all the facts. He felt it best to come back and check on them later and decide then what to do.

***

Luke opened the back door, dropped his book bag on the kitchen floor, kicked off his shoes and reached for the biscuit tin.

"Erm, did you forget something?" said Mum,

suddenly appearing from the pantry.

Luke stuck his feet back in his shoes and shuffled them out of the kitchen.

"Sohhy," he said, his mouth full of gingernut.

"Don't tread the heels down!" she reminded him wearily, "and that's not what I meant."

He looked back, confused, and then noticed his book bag.

"Sorry," he said again, picked it up and started to walk away.

"That's not what I meant," she said again, in a sort of sing-songy tone of voice.

Luke stood still. He was tired. It had been a long day. Could she not just tell him what she meant? Did they have to go through this trial and error game every time? He turned to look at her.

"What?" he asked, "what did you mean?"

Mum gave him a look which meant he should

Luke Walker and the new teacher

modify his look. He did. Then she told him.

"Shouldn't you ask before you take a biscuit?"

"Can I have a biscuit please?"

"You may have two biscuits," she said smiling, "how was your first day back? Did you like your new teacher?"

Luke slumped into a chair in the dining room.

"He's alright," he said unenthusiastically.

"He? I thought you'd be with Ms Robinson this year."

"Yeah. So did I."

"So, how come you're not? Who are you with? Mr Green?"

"No. A new one. Mr Beardsley."

"Oh. What's he like?"

Luke appreciated his mother's interest but really wasn't in the mood to recap the day's events.

Luke Walker and the new teacher

"He's alright," he said again, "I've got to do me homework," and he lifted himself sluggishly from the chair and headed upstairs to cover his new books.

***

On Wednesday afternoon Luke was able to find Joe at the end of school.

"What's it like in Muz Robinson's class?" he asked jealously.

"s'alright," said Joe.

Luke was surprised to get such a tepid response but realised that Joe was just being considerate, not wanting to rub it in. He appreciated that and gladly changed the subject.

"We need to go home by the main road," he told his friend, "I've got to check on some sheep."

When they got there Luke was very concerned to see they were just as he'd left them the day before.

"They must be so hungry," he said, "and thirsty."

The boys crossed the road. Joe was equally worried.

"We should let 'em back into the field," he suggested, "there's grass; and a water trough."

"Yeah, I think so too," said Luke, "but I can't open the gate coz o' the padlock." He tugged pointlessly at the hardened steel lock. "Where's the farmer got to? I thought he would 'ave let 'em out by now."

"P'rhaps he's had an accident," Joe said anxiously, "he might be dead!"

Luke hadn't thought of that.

"Oh no! He prob'ly dint tell no one he'd locked the sheep up without food 'n' water, and if he's dead, no one'll know they're here, and they'll starve to death!" His eyes were wide with alarm.

"Call the RSPCA!" said Joe suddenly, "this is cruelty to animals, lockin' em up without food or water! The RSPCA'll rescue 'em!"

"Yesss!" said Luke and the two of them rushed back to his house.

Luke found the number in the phone book and decided, for privacy, to use the phone in his mum's bedroom. He put it on speaker so that Joe could hear. It rang for a few seconds before being answered by a recorded message.

"Thank you for calling the RSPCA. Please note some calls may be recorded for training and monitoring purposes. To proceed press 1 now."

Luke pressed 1.

"Thank you. Please say your postcode."

Luke was flummoxed.

"What's my postcode?" he mouthed to Joe.

Joe shrugged.

The recording tried again.

Luke Walker and the new teacher

"Please say your postcode out loud or key it into the keypad."

Luke pressed some random keys.

"Thank you. Now please key in your house number."

He pressed the seven and the one.

"Thank you. Your address is 71 Broomhill Drive, Glasgow, Scotland. If this is correct press 1; if this is incorrect press 2; press 3 to return to the main menu."

Luke was exasperated. No, it wasn't correct but he wasn't going to tell them that or he'd have to start all over again. He pressed 1.

"Thank you. Now say your name out loud."

"Robin Locksley."

"Thank you. If you have called because of an animal in distress, please choose between the following options: If you're worried about a dog in a hot car, press 1. If you've found an abandoned ..."

Luke threw his head back in frustration.

"We 'aven't got time for this! Jus' let me talk ta someone!"

"It's a good job you're not on a mobile," Joe agreed, "Janet's always runnin' out of credit on hers."

The machine listed several options before concluding with:

"For anything else, please hold for an operator."

"Finally," Luke mouthed and the ring tone began again. After a minute or so, a live person answered.

"Thank you for calling the RSPCA. How may I help you?"

"There's some sheep locked in a muddy paddock with no food or water," Luke told her.

"Are they in distress?"

"Wun't you be distressed if you hadn't

eaten anythin' for a whole day an' night? Or drunken anythin'?"

"It's only been one day?"

"And a night. More 'n that now," Luke said.

"Are they injured? Do they look like they've been abused or neglected."

"Well, no, they don't seem to be injured."

"I'm sorry but I don't think any of our inspectors will come out if they're not injured or in distress."

"They haven't had anythin' to drink or eat since yesterday! They're really hungry and they're locked in there! You've got to let 'em out!"

"I'm sorry. Perhaps you can ask the farmer to check on them. Do you know who the sheep belong to?"

"We think the farmer might be dead."

"Who are you talking to?" Mum stood in the doorway.

Luke disconnected the call.

"Nobody. We was jus' pretendin'," he thought it best not to involve Mum.

"I heard a woman's voice. Who were you talking to?" she persisted.

"Somebody. Don't matter who."

"I beg your pardon? You're in my room, using my phone and I insist you tell me who you were speaking to!"

Luke looked momentarily at the floor and then back at her.

"Joe's mum," he lied again, "she said Joe could stay for tea. We're goin' to check on Curly and Squirt."

Mrs Walker decided to pretend she believed him.

"Okay," she consented, "back by six please. And in future, ask before you use the phone."

While Mum stayed in her room to sort the laundry, Luke and Joe rushed downstairs.

Luke Walker and the new teacher

"We'll feed 'em ourselves!" Luke decided.

He handed a shopping bag to Joe and opened the fridge. Luckily, Mum had just been shopping.

"Take these," he said, "and these, and these," and he handed him about twenty carrots, two cucumbers, a cabbage, a lettuce and sixteen apples. The bag was heavy. Luke grabbed another one to share Joe's burden and they left.

When they got to the bus stop they stood under the shelter and looked carefully in every direction to make sure no one was watching. Then they hurried across the road and emptied their bags into the muddy paddock. The sheep didn't trust the boys and they crowded against the opposite fence.

"These'll give 'em water as well as food," said Luke, "I hope they like 'em." He was a little disappointed that they didn't seem too keen to tuck in.

"I think they're frightened of us," Joe suggested, "p'rhaps we should go back over the road and watch from there."

Luke agreed and within a few minutes the sheep bravely and hungrily partook. The boys were extremely relieved.

"That's good," said Joe, "we'll jus' feed 'em every day 'til they let 'em out."

"Yeah, but tomorrow we'll get the food from your house or my mum'll catch on."

"Okay."

Then they went to visit Curly and Squirt, before popping in to Joe's house to tell his mum that he was going to tea at Luke's.

***

On Thursday Mr Beardsley said that Year 5 were going to be responsible for the Christmas concert this year. He said they were going to put on a musical production of A Christmas

Carol by Charles Dickens.

"... so for any of you who are aspiring singers or actors, the auditions are being held on Friday after school."

This was interesting. It was a good story. The Muppet Christmas Carol was one of Luke's favourite films. He'd never thought of himself as an actor and the idea of performing did not really appeal to him. However, when Jared was in the school play a couple of years ago he said they had to rehearse so much that he missed loads of lessons.

"What parts?" he blurted out suddenly without thinking. Mr Beardsley was writing on the board.

"I'm sorry?"

Luke felt a bit embarrassed.

"er, sorry, what parts are in the play?"

"Oh, er, well, lots. Scrooge, Scrooge's nephew, Bob Cratchit, the Spirits, Tiny Tim, ..."

"They're all boy parts," said Tania Spriggs, one of the new girls. She was understandably disgruntled.

"Oh, there's lots of girls' parts too," said Mr Beardsley, trying to think of one. "Oh, er, there's Mrs Cratchit, and er, the Cratchit daughters, and Scrooge's sister, Scrooge's nephew's wife," he was on a roll now. But then he realised he wasn't. He couldn't think of any more.

Tania huffed.

"The wife, the sister, the daughter! All minor roles!" she said, dispirited, "I look forward to a school play with a strong female lead!"

"I tell you what, talk to Ms Robinson at the auditions. She's adapting the story into a script so I'm sure she'll make sure there's plenty of good roles to be had for both sexes."

Luke gave it some more thought. He liked the idea of being one of the spirits. The really scary one.

Mr Beardsley resumed writing on the board. Maths. Again. Luke pictured himself as the Ghost of Christmas Yet To Come. He'd have a long, black, hooded cape; his face would be painted white with black cavernous eyes; he'd have sharp talons for fingernails and ...

"Luke. What's next?"

Luke, brought abruptly from his reverie, had no idea what was being asked of him. His bewilderment was visible. Mr Beardsley banged the pen on the board to draw Luke's attention to the sum written there.

"Four thousand, two hundred and seventy nine divided by twenty two. Long division. Max did the first part. What's next?"

Luke shook his head. He really hated it when someone interrupted his train of thought. He was in the middle of something. What was it? He turned to ask Joe but Joe wasn't there. Oh yes, the Ghost of Christmas Yet To Come, that was the part for him. Then he had another thought. If Joe was in it too they'd be together again. He wondered what part Joe would like. Mr Beardsley moved on to Katia. She didn't know either.

***

On their way home from school Luke and Joe discussed the Christmas concert.

"I don't wanna be in it," said Joe.

"You could just 'ave a small part," Luke suggested, "then we'd be together."

"Oh yeah," said Joe, but his heart wasn't in it. He was terrified at the thought of being on stage; of being watched by people. Luke sympathised and racked his brains for a way that Joe could be part of the production without actually having to be on stage. Then it came to him.

"You could be the scenery painter!" he said

with great satisfaction. "Then you'd 'ave to be there, paintin' the scenes while we're rehearsin'. Then I could chat to you when it's not my scene and I could help you. I could fetch your pens and paints and brushes. You could tell 'em I'm your assistant so they don't send me back to lessons when it's not my scene."

It was a brilliant plan. Joe was as happy about it as Luke.

They ducked into Joe's house for sheep food. His mum was in the kitchen.

"Hello Joe, oh, and hello Luke. Are we returning the favour tonight then?" she asked.

"What d'you mean?" said Joe, trying to think of a way to entice her from the kitchen.

"Is Luke staying here for tea today?"

"Oh, er, no. Thank you," said Luke, "I've jus' come to borra somethin'."

That gave Joe an idea.

"Yeah, I want to lend 'im my book about

trains," he said, "ya know, the one Auntie Sue gave me."

"Okay," said his mum without looking up from the potatoes she was peeling.

"on'y," said Joe, tentatively, "I don't know where it is. Could you find it for me?"

"Haven't I got enough to do?" she said indignantly, "what else do you want - shall I tie your shoelaces? Shall I clean your teeth for you?"

Joe shook his head.

"Find it yourself you cheeky beggar!" she concluded, and that was that.

The boys stepped back outside. It was no use. She'd started the dinner which meant she'd be in there for at least another hour.

"Sorry," said Joe, "we'll have to get somethin' from yours again."

"There's nothin' left to take," said Luke, "Mum said we'll have to have tinned veg 'til she

Luke Walker and the new teacher

can get to the shops again and coz she thinks I took it for Curly and Squirt and the damsons - typical! They always blame me! - she won't let me watch telly for a week!"

The boys looked at each other and thought hard. There had to be a way to get something to eat for those poor starving sheep.

"Where there's a will, there's a way," said Luke, not for the first time. Then he had a thought. An idea. A good one. It might be tricky but it was do-able.

"Remember that farm behind the pony field, next to the rec?"

"Yes," said Joe.

"They grow salads and things, in them plastic tunnels."

"Mmm," said Joe, nervously.

"So, I've seen 'em, them tunnels, all they 'ave to do is water 'em twice a day. The rest of the time there's no one in 'em."

"But they've got them big dogs,"

"Okay, well, we'll take a couple o' dog toys, and then you can distract ..."

Joe shook his head.

"I don't want to distract."

"Okay, I'll distract 'em and you can go into the tunnels to get the salad."

"That's stealin'."

"To save lives!" Luke reminded him, "and anyway, they've prob'ly got hundreds o' lettuces and cucumbers, they won't miss a few."

Taking Joe's silence as tacit consent, Luke continued.

"First, we'll go to mine to get the dog toys; and a bag; then we'll go to the farm and I'll climb in to play with the dogs; as soon as I've got their 'ttention, you sneak into the ..."

Joe laughed.

"What?" said Luke, annoyed that his great

plan was a source of amusement.

"Look over there," said Joe, pointing to the bottom of his garden.

There stood two heavily laden apple trees.

"Or," said Luke, "we could take some apples."

They emptied the contents of their school bags behind the water butt and replaced them with apples. With no time to lose, they headed to the muddy paddock.

They weren't prepared for what they found. Parked in the field, alongside the still confined sheep, was a double decker lorry.

The top deck was already full of sheep.

The farmer was there, with his dogs, talking to the lorry driver. It was clear to the boys what was about to happen. That's why they were locked up there. They were waiting for transport. Waiting to be taken to their deaths. Luke and Joe stood frozen at the bus shelter. They dropped their bags of apples.

"The lorry must be late," said Joe in a husky whisper.

"Why?"

"Coz they haven't been fed for two days, they must've not known it was gonna be that long."

"It's not late!" snapped Luke angrily, "look how clean an' shiny that lorry is! I bet they don't wanna get their lorry dirty - they don't want no poo and wee in their lorry so they don't let 'em eat or drink before the journey. Their last journey!"

Joe felt a lump in his throat and his heart

ached.

"That's horrible!" he said desperately, "what can we do? We've got to do something!"

Luke's eyes started to sting as he watched them send in the dogs to herd the hungry sheep onto the lorry. He picked up the biggest stone he could find and threw it as hard as he could at the lorry's windscreen across the road. It missed.

"There's nothin' we can do!" he said, grabbing his bag of apples, "unless you've got a thousand pounds to pay the farmer for 'em, and a hundred allotments to keep 'em on!"

Still they hated themselves for doing nothing and walked away in silent misery.

**

Friday morning at breakfast, Luke's dad observed how cold and wet it was.

"It's big coat weather already," he told his wife, "it's amazing how quick the temperature

Luke Walker and the new teacher

drops once September arrives."

"Sometimes," Mum agreed, "it'll probably be warm again tomorrow." She looked at her boys. "Your big coats need a wash to freshen them up," she remembered, "so you'll have to wear an extra jumper under your summer jackets for now."

"I'm not wearin' that wool jumper!" said Luke firmly.

"Luke, it's cold. If your Dad says it's cold then you know it is. He's usually hotter than the rest of us."

"Than you," Dad corrected her.

"Yeah," Jared agreed, "you're the one who's always cold," he laughed.

"Well then, there you go, so if Dad thinks it's cold ..."

"I'm not wearin' that jumper! Take it back an' get your money back! We're not givin' money to farmers!"

Luke Walker and the new teacher

Everyone stopped eating. Dad was not impressed.

"Luke Eugene Walker, how dare you speak to your mother like that? Apologise right now!" He spoke in that slow, quiet, angry way that meant you'd gone too far. Luke realised he shouldn't be taking it out on Mum.

"Sorry," he said quietly, "but I don't want you to pay money to sheep farmers. I hate farmers!"

Mum's response was gentle.

"Luke, clearly something has upset you, but the fact remains, as I told you, that wool isn't cruel. It doesn't hurt them to be sheared."

Luke tried to explain it to her in a way she would understand.

"It doesn't make any difference," he said, "they kill 'em anyway."

"Not for wool they don't. They kill animals for leather but not for wool."

Luke Walker and the new teacher

"They kill 'em anyway," Luke said again, "they make money out of 'em for wool; then they kill 'em and make money out of 'em for meat. They kill 'em for money and they're horrible, nasty, evil, criminal murderers and I don't want you to give them any of our money!"

Nobody could argue with that.

"Okay," said Mum, "I'll take it back today."

***

Joe gave Luke back the books and pens he'd left in his garden the day before.

"I forgot them last night," he apologised.

"Me too," said Luke, taking possession of three brand new, very soggy, text books, and two exercise books in which a lot of his work had dissolved.

"Put them on the radiator," Joe suggested helpfully.

"Yeah," said Luke.

The bell rang and they went their separate

ways.

At half past three, all the Year Fives who wanted to be in the Christmas concert went to the hall to audition for Ms Robinson and Mr Beardsley. There were more parts available than actors to play them so Luke felt confident he'd get something. He was expecting to have to get up on stage and recite a line or two from the play, as he'd seen done in a movie once. However, when Ms Robinson saw how few people had turned up she simply asked for a show of hands for each role. If only one person raised their hand for a particular role, they got it. If more than one person raised their hand, Mr Beardsley drew one of their names from a hat. Luke felt this diminished the accomplishment somewhat. He was the only applicant for the role of Third Spirit so the part was his, in addition he was pressed to play Jacob Marley which he was happy to do. Simon

Butler would play Ebenezer Scrooge as an old man, a young man and a child. Katia got the parts of young Scrooge's sweetheart and Mrs Cratchit; Kenny got Bob Cratchit, Fezziwig and the coachman; Tania wanted to play Scrooge's nephew and Scrooge's sister because she thought it would add realism to have some discernible family resemblance between those characters. Her wish was granted. And so it went on. Children were permitted to leave after their roles were assigned and by a quarter past five only a few minor roles remained to be cast. Joe and Luke were the only children left in the hall. Luke was waiting for Joe who, for almost two hours, had waited patiently for an opportunity to ask if he could paint the scenery. He had brought with him some preliminary sketches of ideas for backdrops and costumes but when he approached Ms Robinson, she misunderstood his reason for being there.

"Okay Joe, that leaves us with Scrooge's servant, the Gentleman Visitor, the Cook, and the Butcher. Do you think you can handle those?"

Joe went white in the face.

"er, no, he don't want them," said Luke, stepping in.

"Excuse me, I was talking to Joe," said Ms Robinson, quite testily. "Come on Joe, they're only small parts, you can do those for me can't you?"

Joe looked at the sketchbook in his hands.

"I brought these ..." he mumbled nervously.

"What was that? You'll do it? Thank you Joe," and she wrote his name next to the character names on her clipboard.

Joe looked at Luke with panic in his eyes.

"No, he's not doin' the actin', he's good at paintin' scenery. He'll be too busy paintin' to do any actin'," said Luke persuasively.

Ms Robinson looked at Luke as if her patience was at an end.

"This is nothing to do with you. If Joe didn't want to do it he would have said so. Please credit him with enough intelligence to speak for himself and stop interfering." She turned back to Joe. "Okay Joe?"

Joe nodded his assent.

Ms Robinson closed her clipboard and began to pack up her things. Luke knew full well that Joe was only there because he'd asked him to be. He couldn't let him get lumbered with this.

"No," he said with determination "Joe don't wanna do it. That's not why he came. He daren't say it coz you're in a mood, but he definitely don't wanna do it!"

Ms Robinson glared at him in that all too familiar way.

Luke Walker and the new teacher

"Luke. Walker," she said slowly as if something had just occurred to her, "you're the one Cathy Tebbut warned me about."

At this point Mr Beardsley, who had witnessed the entire interaction, decided it was time to intervene.

"Can I have a word Ms Robinson?" he asked.

She glared again at Luke and then stepped aside to speak to her colleague. Luke sat down on the floor next to Joe.

"Sorry," he said.

"S'oright," his friend replied.

After a few minutes of hushed discussion Ms Robinson left. Mr Beardsley walked over to the boys.

"Ms Robinson and I have been thinking," he said, "it doesn't work very well to have an odd number of pupils in a class because when we need you to work with a partner, there's always an odd one out."

Luke Walker and the new teacher

The boys nodded. That was true.

"So," Mr Beardsley went on, "it's better to have twenty six or twenty four pupils in a class than twenty five."

The boys nodded again.

"So, Ms Robinson has agreed that it would be a good idea for you to transfer to my class Joe, if that's alright with you."

Joe's now very enthusiastic nod was accompanied by a wide smile. Luke smiled too.

"Okay then," said Mr Beardsley, smiling back at them, "I'll see you both, ten to nine, on Monday." He started to turn away before adding, "oh, and Joe, Ms Robinson said she'd be delighted to have your help with the scenery because she's going to give some of the Year 4 kids the opportunity to audition for the minor roles."

He winked and walked away.

Chapter Thirteen:

Luke Walker and the Harvest Festival

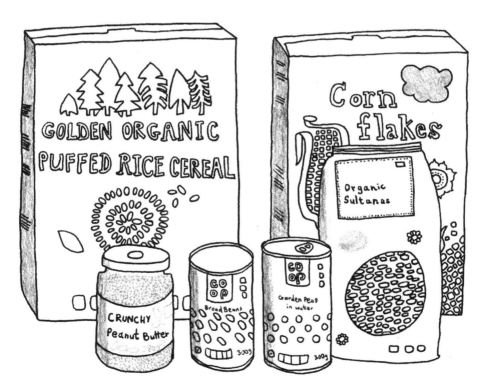

Luke Walker and the Harvest Festival

"And then what happened? Luke?"

"Erm,"

"Weren't you listening? What happened in the end?"

"Oh, um, in the end she saved 'em all, and then they saw she was a girl, coz they thought she was a man before, but they didn't kill 'er because she'd saved China."

Eric, the Sunday School teacher, looked at Luke blankly, as if he wasn't there.

"Mulan? Are you talking about Mulan?" he asked after a long pause.

Luke wondered, not for the first time, why his mum insisted he came to Sunday School to listen to a man who seemed unable to remember, from one minute to the next, what he was supposed to be teaching them.

"Yeah. Mulan. Who saved China from invaders. Remember? Who you've bin tellin' us about."

Luke Walker and the Harvest Festival

"Okay Luke, well, you are clearly capable of paying attention - to Disney films anyway - but you've obviously not heard a word I've said today. I've actually been talking about Miriam, Moses's sister, who hid him in the bulrushes as a baby, and later helped her brother lead the Jews out of Egypt."

Luke frowned in deep thought.

"Oh," he responded at last.

Eric turned to the other seven children in his charge and continued. Luke resented the 'I give up' look that Eric's features expressed before they withdrew. He'd seen it many times. It was uncalled for.

"Mulan. Miriam. They're both ancient. They're both women. They both saved a whole country. They're both heroes. They both start with an M. Anyone could easily get them mixed up," he thought as he leafed through the parish magazine.

Luke Walker and the Harvest Festival

At last he heard the final hymn being sung by the grown-ups in the room next door and he unhooked his jacket from its peg.

"Hold your horses Luke," Eric recalled him to the group. "You can go when your parents come for you but remember that next week is Harvest Festival so I'd like all of you to be here at ten o'clock on Saturday to help me decorate the Sunday School room. The church secretary told me that the committee has decided to do things differently this year... blah blah blah ..."

"Saturday? Not likely!" thought Luke. He could hear the scraping back of chairs and the hubbub of grown-ups talking, getting gradually louder. Any minute now the blue door would swing open and Mum would effect his release. Any minute now.

Eric finished whatever he was saying, Luke slipped his arms into his jacket sleeves, the

Luke Walker and the Harvest Festival

door opened, and he hurried towards it.

"Bye Luke," Eric called after him, "See you Saturday."

"Bye," he replied without looking back.

***

At school on Monday Luke noticed a familiar theme. Mr Beardsley had written on the board:

Harvest Festival

He concluded that either Mr Beardsley had copied his project idea from Eric or Eric got it from him. This was no bad thing. He could get two for one. Score points with the same work twice.

Mr Beardsley explained that they should all bring in donations of food this week to make a Harvest Festival display in the school hall. Then they would have a special afternoon assembly on Friday to thank God for the harvest. As the food would later be donated to the homeless shelter in town he requested no perishables, only tins and packeted dry goods please.

So Luke went home that afternoon and explained to Mum what he needed for the Harvest festivals.

"Looks like I won't be able to do it once and hand it in twice though, coz they're givin' all the school festival food to the homeless shelter so I'll need another lot for Sunday School. Tins and dry stuff he said. Have we got any of that?"

Mum looked in the pantry. "Yes, we've got some dried lentils and pasta, and some tinned beans you can have. I'll get something for the church harvest when I go shopping. Tins again I think, otherwise it'll smell."

"What will?"

"The fish."

"Whaddaya mean fish? Why are you gettin'

fish?"

"Didn't Eric tell you? The chapel committee want to do a different kind of Harvest Festival this year. Instead of the usual fruits, vegetables, grains and bread etcetera etcetera, they want to do a display of the harvest of the sea."

"What?!" Luke could hardly believe it. "They're proud of killin' sea animals are they? They want to show off about killin' God's creatures do they? That's very Christian - I don't think!"

"Well, Luke," Mum tried to calm him down, "I know you don't like it sweetheart but Jesus ate fish didn't he? Some of his disciples were fishermen."

Luke was unconvinced.

"How do we know that? Just coz someone wrote it in a book thousands of years ago in a diffrent language. P'rhaps they din't translate it right. P'rhaps they din't tell the truth.

Luke Walker and the Harvest Festival

Prob'ly whoever wrote it wasn't even there at the time so they wouldn't even know!" He was gaining momentum. "And, Jesus was perfect," he went on, "so he wun't 'ave done somethin' that hurt someone else on purpose. And he told them disciples to stop bein' fishermen din't he? And he wun't 'ave done that if he thought they were doin' a good thing. And Jesus said God cares about every sparrow so if he cares about every sparrow then he definitely cares about every fish and he said 'thou shalt not kill' so he couldn't be clearer than that!"

Red in the face from talking so fast without taking a breath and satisfied he'd settled the point, Luke stomped out of the room. Mrs Walker winced as the hall door slammed and Luke's heavy footsteps pounded the stairs. She held her breath until all was quiet and then, just as she relaxed back into scrubbing potatoes, her son's face re-appeared

Luke Walker and the Harvest Festival

around the door.

"Oh!" she gasped, "you made me jump."

"Don't get any fish," he entreated, "please."

The following morning at breakfast Luke was distracted. He made no argument when Jared consumed the last of the frosted flakes; he didn't defend himself when Dad told him off for knocking over the sugar bowl even though it was actually Jared who'd done it in his haste to grab the frosted flakes. The rest of the family were too busy to notice, but Luke was not himself. Eventually, when Jared and Dad had left for the day and Luke was left alone with Mum he told her,

"I've decided I don't want to go to Sunday School any more."

"Well I know you don't want to go Luke, but you're going. It's good for you. I want you to learn good values, to be a good boy," she responded firmly.

"I've got good values!" said Luke, indignant. "What do you mean values?" he added.

Mum sighed.

"Oh Luke, being a Christian means being good and kind and respecting your father and mother and not stealing and not lying, things like that," she explained, "doing as you're told," she added.

"And not killin'," said Luke.

"Of course not killing Luke, that goes without saying,"

"But they're killin'! They're celebratin' killin'

Luke Walker and the Harvest Festival

fish and if that's Christian I don't want to be it!"

"Oh Luke why do you have to get so angry over these things? You might not want them to eat fish but they do. People do. People always have. And so do bears and cats and birds, and even other fish Luke. It's the way of the world and there's nothing you can do about it."

"I don't want to go! I'm not going!" he insisted. Mum inhaled deeply and counted to ten.

"Fine. But you are not going to just disappear like a coward without telling them why. You've got to be grown up about it and make it clear to Eric why this sea harvest upsets you."

Luke sulked. He was not a coward. He wasn't afraid of anything. They walked to school in silence, Luke was deep in thought. When they entered the school gates they were almost run over by Simon Butler racing across their path on his new bike and then, when he knew he'd got their attention, he pulled a wheelie.

"He's a bit of a show-off that one," said Mum, amused.

Luke snorted.

"A bit?!" he scoffed, "more like a lot! He's a lot of a show-off. He's pretty much all show-off! There's nothing else to 'im. 'cept idiot. And creep. He's a idiot creep show-off!" Luke concluded decisively.

Mum chuckled.

"Boys will be boys," she said, "he's just making a point. He's just making it clear to everyone watching that he's good at that."

***

All morning, while Mr Beardsley was talking about the ancient Greeks, Luke was thinking about what Mum had told him to do. He considered very carefully exactly what she'd

Luke Walker and the Harvest Festival

said and by the time Dionysus had whisked Ariadne away from Theseus he was satisfied that he could do as he was told without compromising his prince pauls. He'd need Joe's help.

At 3.47pm Luke and Joe stood in Curly and Squirt's shed. There was a big old wooden ottoman at the back. Joe had never noticed it before because ordinarily Luke kept a bale of hay on top of it and the whole lot was usually covered with a tatty blue tarpaulin. Luke started to lift the lid and then hesitated, looking over his shoulder to make sure the shed door was shut. It was.

"This is where I keep the stuff I've constigated on holiday," he told his trusted friend, confidentially.

Joe looked puzzled. Luke put him in the picture.

"Remember me Nan and Grandad's got a

caravan at the seaside where there's fishing boats on the beach? Remember I told you?"

Joe nodded.

"Well," Luke went on, "whenever we go there I look out for things on the beach wot need takin' outer circle-ation. Dangerous things."

"And you constigate them?" Joe asked with the appearance of comprehension.

"Mm. Well, some I jus' find, abandoned. Some I constigate from people wot are doin' horrible things with 'em."

Joe peered inside the trunk but wasn't sure exactly what he was looking at. It was a miscellaneous jumble of what looked like rubbish - bits of plastic, rope, cord, wood, wire. All very unpleasant and dirty. It stank.

"And now you want to move it somewhere else?" Joe tried hard to make sense of the little Luke had told him so far.

"Yeah. On'y it's too much stuff for one

trip with just me. Your mum's got one o' them shopping trolley-bag things, and mine's got two, an old one and a new one - I reckon we could fit all this stuff into them and move it without anyone bein' able to see what we've got. They'll just think we've done the shoppin' for our mums."

Joe nodded.

"Okaaay."

"And," Luke went on, "can you get any left over paint off your dad? Somethin' he wun't miss? Somethin' he's finished with and wun't mind you havin'. Somethin' he would rather you dint bother 'im by askin' for. Somethin' he'd be pleased you took off 'is hands without botherin' 'im. Somethin' reddish."

Joe wondered.

"I'll see what I can do."

***

Saturday was the day that Luke always helped Dad on the allotment and today, more than ever before, he was very glad of it. It gave him the perfect excuse not to help decorate the Sunday school room for the Harvest Festival. He remembered they were meeting at 10 o'clock and imagined that it wouldn't take them more than an hour or two so they'd be done by lunch time. Then the ladies on the cleaning and flowers rota were going to decorate the chapel. Mum was one of those ladies and she got home at twenty past four.

"Put the kettle on love," she called to her husband, "and if you look in the pantry I've a feeling you might find a packet of chocolate hobnobs behind the teabags."

"Well, half a packet anyway," Luke's dad grinned as he nodded towards the dining table where six or seven of them adorned a small plate. Mrs Walker dropped exhausted into a chair.

"I knew there was a reason I married you," she smiled as he handed her a hot cup of tea and sat down with one himself. "Thank you love," she said, "that whole afternoon was an uphill struggle. Mrs Kirby was complaining the whole time that she thought we should be doing the traditional Harvest Festival display of fruits and breads and stuff, and Mabel was arguing that change was good and we should embrace change and move with the times. What's modern about fishing I do not know! And then

Luke Walker and the Harvest Festival

every time they stopped arguing Gordon would get them going again with 'I suppose we have to do what the committee decides, never mind what the rest of the congregation wants!' I don't know what was more exhausting - scrubbing the kitchen floor or listening to ...."

"Shhh," Mr Walker interrupted, "forget about all that now, it's done. Drink your tea."

"Don't shush me!" Mum snapped. She hated it when he did that.

"I was just saying don't worry about it, calm down ...." He never learned.

"I am calm! I'm not worried, I was just telling you what happened! I don't like being shushed!"

"I'm with Mrs Kirby," thought Luke as he took advantage of his parents bickering and swiped the chapel keys from Mum's bag before heading for the front door.

"Jus' goin' to check on Curly and Squirt," he

called.

"Home by six!" Mum called after him.

"Six?!" he thought, grabbing the shoppers from the hall cupboard and hurrying out.

It was just after five when Joe and Luke arrived at the chapel gate. Luckily no one was around to hear its metal hinges squeal. They slunk across the lawn past the large wooden crucifix with the spikes on top to stop pigeons landing on it, and Luke unlocked the heavy door.

In the Sunday School room Luke was unsurprised to find quaint and colourful cardboard fishing boats stuck to a massive collage that covered a whole wall. The boats were manned by friendly fishermen pulling up nets by hand. The water beneath them was gleaming turquoise and filled with colourful fish who looked only too eager to swim into the welcoming nets. A golden beach was pictured behind with market stalls where smiling

Luke Walker and the Harvest Festival

fishmongers sold fish to happy villagers under a soft blue sky. A red and white striped lighthouse kindly warned the fishermen to stay away from the rocks. And across the sky large paper letters spelled out the words:

THANK YOU HEAVENLY FATHER FOR YOUR BOUNTY IN THE SEA

"Typical!" said Luke with contempt and uncharacteristic brevity. There was no time for lengthy verbal condemnations. They just got on with it.

Forty-six minutes later Joe was on his way home with gratitude as Luke dropped the last armful of tinned fish into the wheelie bin behind the building. Tomorrow there'd be no Joe.

Luke Walker and the Harvest Festival

Tomorrow Luke would be on his own. Which wasn't a problem, because he wasn't a coward.

***

Luke was quiet at breakfast on Sunday and Mum sympathised.

"You're very preoccupied this morning Luke, are you worried about talking to Eric?"

"Er, kind of," Luke admitted.

"Mm, it's never easy to tell someone something they don't want to hear but it's better to be honest."

"Yeah," said Luke, enlivened by a slight resurgence in confidence, "it's better if they know the truth."

At ten to ten, Luke and his mum approached the chapel gate. Mrs Walker wondered what was going on. People were standing around on the lawn outside and the village bobby was there, talking to the minister.

"What's going on?" she asked Gordon.

Luke Walker and the Harvest Festival

"Vandalism," he said, flatly, "a horrible mess."

"Oh no! How awful!" she said and rushed in.

Luke followed at a cautious distance. Mabel, standing in the doorway, advised Mum not to enter.

"All our work yesterday - ruined!" she mourned, "it's a horror show in there!"

When Mrs Walker stepped forward the first thing to strike her was the awful smell. She shielded her nose with her hand. Draped over the pulpit was a huge, orange, fishing net, tangled, filthy and stinking with rotten seaweed and the small fish and crustacean victims who'd been trapped and strangled by it long after the fleet had left it to drift untethered. The communion table and the floor around it exhibited a collection of old lobster pots and traps, a mess of wire and barbed hooks, a couple of rusty knives and a matching set of hooks, pliers and other fishmonger blades that looked hardly used.

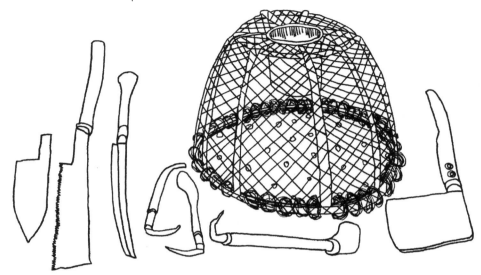

These were set off to best advantage by numerous anchovy and sardine corpses variously strewn and interwoven throughout. The whole ensemble was liberally splattered with what looked like blood.

Eric emerged from the Sunday School room.

"There's more in here," he told her.

Mrs Walker had a bad feeling.

Apprehensively she followed Eric into the Sunday School room and discovered the picturesque fishing village scene was no more. There were no fish, no happy villagers and no fishmongers; the lighthouse had fallen into the sea and the colourful fishing boats had crashed into the rocks. Some of the paper letters had been rearranged across the sky to spell

THOU SHALT NOT KILL

"I told you we should have done the normal fruit and vegetable display!" Mrs Kirby chimed in authoritatively, "I said to the minister last week - people want a traditional harvest festival with fruits and vegetables and golden sheaves of wheat. Genesis 1, verse 29: I have provided all kinds of grain and fruit for you to eat," she quoted, "This is a message from God!"

Mabel was irritated.

"God didn't do this!"

"Whoever did it was sent by Him!" retorted

Mrs Kirby, and no one dared disagree.

***

Mrs Walker kept her anger buttoned down. She didn't say anything until they were well out of earshot of the other church-goers. It would be too shameful if anyone else knew what she suspected. Not to mention Luke might get a criminal record. Eventually, when they were almost home, she asked coldly,

"Who do you think did it Luke?"

"I'm with Mrs Kirby," he answered honestly, "whoever did it was sent by God."

Chapter fourteen:

Luke Walker and the Halloween party

Luke Walker and the Halloween party

Luke, Joe, Isabel and Tania looked at the circle and gasped. They hadn't believed it could happen. Now that it had, they were scared.

"That's it then," said Luke eventually, "I'll prob'ly be dead by Christmas."

***

Three days earlier everything had seemed so ordinary. Boringly so. Class 5A were doing History. History was sometimes interesting, sometimes exciting and often-times boring. This particular lesson seemed like it was going to fit into the last category. Mr Beardsley was talking whilst writing on the board, which meant he had his back to the class, which meant very few people were even pretending to listen.

"... historians believe that many of these traditions originate from Celtic harvest festivals, but others are of the opinion that it has always been a Christian ...."

Luke Walker and the Halloween party

"T," whispered Luke.

"No," said Joe, as he drew a diagonal support on the gallows.

"F,"

"Yes," said Joe and filled in the Fs.

"Ooh, two Fs! Is it coffee?"

"No," and he drew the noose.

Mr Beardsley rambled on and Luke found it disturbed his concentration. He felt sure he was close. There couldn't be that many words with double F. Then the teacher said something that caught his attention.

"... Christians historically abstained from meat on All Hallows' Eve, which is why it was traditional to eat certain vegetarian foods on this special day. In particular they ate apples, potato pancakes, and soul cakes.

"What's he talkin' about?" Luke asked Joe.

Joe looked at him blankly. Isabel Jessop tapped him on the shoulder and passed him a note which said 'Halloween'.

Luke nodded a thank you to her. He pushed the note across to Joe.

"Halloween is a veggietareun day! We'd better listen coz he might want us to explain things to the others."

Joe nodded and smiled uncomfortably. He'd never been called upon to explain anything to anyone and the idea didn't appeal to him. However, realising that if any explanations were needed his friend would certainly provide them, he regained his composure. The boys watched their teacher and listened.

"All Hallows' Eve, otherwise known as All Saints Eve, Allhalloween or, nowadays, just Halloween, begins the three days of Allhallowtide during which people remembered saints and martyrs and other dead people."

"Oh my gosh!" thought Luke, "it seemed like it was gettin' int'restin' so we stopped playin' an' now it's borin' again!"

"... such as roasted sweetcorn, roasted pumpkin seeds, toffee apples,..."

"Toffee! Is it toffee?"

"No," said Joe, drawing the condemned man's circular head.

"... and they would enjoy these foods at Halloween parties where they'd also play some fun games."

Mr Beardsley had their attention again.

"So I thought we could have a Year 5 Halloween party. We'll invite class 5B and play some of these traditional games."

A buzz of excitement filled the room.

"When?" someone shouted.

"On the 31st of October of course. The day after tomorrow. Friday."

"Where?"

"Here. At seven o'clock 'til ten. I'll send a note home to your parents today."

Luke Walker and the Halloween party

Mr Beardsley was so disorganised. Luke liked that about him.

"Will it be fancy dress?"

"Indeed it will, but stop shouting out and let me finish. I'll answer any questions you still have at the end of the lesson."

***

Friday's party was eagerly anticipated by everyone. It was going to be historical. They were going to play traditional games and eat traditional food - which they would have to make from scratch over the next couple of days. Mr Beardsley had given them recipes to take home. And they needed costumes. There was a lot to do and very little time in which to do it. Luke and Joe talked about it while they put on their coats and boots at the end of the day.

"I'm going to be a pirate," said Joe.

"You can't be a pirate, it's not historical."

Luke Walker and the Halloween party

"Isn't it?"

"No, it's made up. Like in Peter Pan."

"Pirates are real," Isabel couldn't help pointing out when she overheard their conversation.

"Not Long John Silver, or Captain Hook, or someone with a parrot on 'is shoulder," Luke clarified.

"What are you comin' as then?" asked Joe.

"William Wilberforce's ghost," said Luke proudly.

"Ooh, good one," said Tania as she returned to Isabel the scarf she'd borrowed. "I'm coming as Queen Elizabeth I," she added, shaking her auburn curls.

"Who can I be?" Isabel wondered aloud.

The girls walked away in deep discussion. Luke and Joe were not far behind. Joe was disappointed that he couldn't go as a pirate.

"What can I go as then?" he asked his

Luke Walker and the Halloween party

friend.

"Go as a lunatic from one of those old asylums," suggested Simon Butler who'd appeared from nowhere, "then you wouldn't need a costume!" And he laughed so loud on his way out that Mrs Tebbut shouted 'PIPE DOWN OUT THERE!' from the classroom next door.

Luke scowled.

"Idiot Butler! Not even s'posed to be in this cloakroom," he hissed under his breath. "Don't worry," he told Joe, "you'll be somethin' better'n 'im!"

***

"Not Mr Darcy! Mr Wilberforce!" Luke insisted. "I don't want to look like some posh bloke from Priden Precipice!"

Mrs Walker pulled the black trousers, white ruffled shirt and long black coat from The Village Players' costume trunk.

"William Wilberforce would have dressed like

Mr Darcy Luke, these will be just the thing," she assured him, "I'll just give them an iron."

"Okay," Luke tentatively agreed, "but what about Joe? Is there anythin' in there that Joe can wear?"

Luke's mum set up the board and plugged in the iron.

"Who's he going as?" she asked.

"Depends what costumes you've got," said Luke, keeping an open mind.

Mum had only recently joined the local amateur dramatics group so she wasn't sure what costumes they'd got. Most of them were a bit worse for wear but they were lucky to be allowed to use them.

"See for yourself," she suggested, "have a rummage and see if anything captures your imagination."

Luke rummaged. Pink tights, brown tights, knickerbockers, caterpillar costume, spider

Luke Walker and the Halloween party

costume, Cheshire Cat costume, blue dress with white pinafore. So far not so good. Red ball gown, green ball gown, yellow ball gown, purple tutu, red clown shoes. Really not good.

"Rubbish!" said Luke ungratefully, "it's all rubbish!"

Mum sighed and switched off the iron.

"Luke - don't just throw them around like that! You're lucky we've been allowed to borrow these," she said, exasperated.

Luke was sorry. He just wanted to find something good for Joe to shut Butler up. He helped Mum pick up the costumes and re-fold them.

"Sorry," he said.

She pressed her lips tight together and looked him in the eye.

"That's alright," she said. Then, just as she was about to put the folded pile back in the trunk, she noticed a couple of things Luke had missed.

"What about these?" she said.

"A nightgown and a Father Christmas beard?" said Luke, unimpressed.

"Not a nightgown, a robe," she explained, "men used to wear these in the olden days, especially in hot countries."

Luke's blank expression indicated he needed another clue.

"Who's that maths guy you like?"

Still blank.

"Vegetarian? Triangles?"

"Pythagoras!"

"Yes!" Mum smiled, "I bet he would have worn something like this. And he probably had a long white beard when he got old."

"Yeah!" Now Luke was excited, "We'll both be veggietareun people from history! Joe can be Pythagoras and I'll be William Wilberforce's ghost!"

Luke Walker and the Halloween party

"Why not just William Wilberforce? Why do you have to be his ghost?"

"Coz it's a Halloween party. Ya know: Hallow-een. It's all about ghosts and scary stuff." He thought his mum would have known that.

"Yes, but you're all going as people from history."

"Yes."

"So they're all dead."

"Yeah." There really was nothing confusing here.

"So why doesn't Joe go as Pythagoras's ghost?"

"It's supposed to be someone who's dead. So he's Pythagoras. The man."

"Yes, I see, so why aren't you the man?"

"I'm going to be William Wilberforce's ghost."

"Not man?"

"No."

Luke Walker and the Halloween party

"But if you're a ghost why isn't Joe going to be a ghost. Or if he's the man, why aren't you the man...?" She caught sight of her own reflection in the mirror and paused, wondering why she kept asking questions to which there could be no satisfactory answer.

"Can you iron this one as well please?" her son asked, handing back the white robe, "I'm goin' to phone Joe and tell 'im."

***

On Friday 31st of October at 7.08 pm, Luke and Joe said goodbye to Luke's dad at the school gate and walked towards the classroom carrying their contributions to the party food. Luke had followed the Halloween recipes given to to him by Mr Beardsley for barm brack (a kind of fruit bread) and colcannon (mashed potatoes mixed with cabbage). Mum had helped a bit. Joe brought the treacle-covered scones he'd made with Janet's assistance, using another of their teacher's traditional recipes. He'd also remembered the string.

Mr Beardsley's classroom was almost unrecognisable.

Hanging from the ceiling were two large imitation crystal chandeliers, covered in cobwebs and emitting a very dim, creamy light. Long dark-purple velvet curtains replaced the Venetian blinds that usually hung in the windows, the bottoms of which sat in folds on the floor around large pumpkins carved with grotesque gargoyle faces.

The boys approached a long table at one end of the room. It was draped in a ragged, dark red table cloth whose dusty hem skimmed the dusty parquet. On it fifteen white candles stood tall on three candelabra, complete with realistic-looking orange and yellow tissue paper flames and untidily littered with long drips of dry wax. Various plates and bowls of food, brought by the children, were set upon the table. Luke and Joe added theirs.

"No, not on there boys," Mr Beardsley startled them, suddenly appearing as he did. "Those are for the games, remember?"

Luke and Joe looked at their teacher and then at each other and laughed. Mr Beardsley had really pulled out all the stops for this party. His already lofty frame appeared even taller than usual, and his apparently-severed head rested in front of his chest, supported by his left arm. Atop the severed head sat an enviable black hat, with wide upturned brim and a sinister-looking white skull and cross-bones on the front.

"Who are you supposed to be?" asked Luke.

"Can't you guess?" teased his teacher, rubbing his brand new coal-black beard.

"No," said Luke. Joe also shook his head. Mr Beardsley tutted.

"Boys, boys boys," he said, shaking his head, "don't you ever listen to my lessons?" he asked rhetorically. "I'm Blackbeard. Remember? The famous pirate who was beheaded in 1718?"

"Pirate?" said Joe, looking daggers at Luke.

Luke decided to change the subject.

"Where shall we put these then?" he asked.

"Not here," said Mr Beardsley, "or they might get eaten. Put them on my desk behind the screen."

The boys did as they were told and made their way through small huddles of various royalty, warriors and poets, a couple of Shakespeares and a Jesus. No sooner had they placed the food on the desk than Mr Beardsley asked Joe to give him the treacle scones and string so that he could set up the game. They would be starting in about ten minutes he told them. Music was already playing and a few people danced self-consciously in the middle of the room.

"This one's for you Joe," came a familiar voice through the speaker when the record changed.

Luke and Joe looked around to see Simon Butler behind a turntable across the room, dressed in a short blonde beard; a gold fitted jacket zipped up to his neck; short gold trousers fastened below the knee; long socks and large-buckled shoes. He thought he was so cool because Mr Beardsley had let him be the DJ. The Lunatics Have Taken Over The Asylum by Fun Boy Three filled the room and Butler laughed excessively at his own joke. Luke and

Joe paid him a visit.

"So glad you took my advice Joe," he said privately, "you look even more like a loon than usual!"

"I'm Pythagoras," said Joe, holding up the right-angled triangle he'd made out of three rulers.

"Oh, yeah, I know you think so, lunatics often think they're somebody famous," he chuckled smugly.

"I'm not a lunatic! I am Pythag..."

"What are you s'posed to be anyway?" Luke interrupted their pointless argument to draw attention to Butler's ridiculous ensemble.

"Sir Walter Raleigh," Butler confessed without shame.

Luke cast his best contemptuous glance at his arch enemy and said nothing.

"Okay, switch the music off now Simon, it's time for the games to begin," Mr Beardsley called

Luke Walker and the Halloween party

across the room.

Mr Beardsley and Thomas had put out four small tables at intervals around the room. They were set up with different traditional Halloween games.

"Take it in turns to play the games at each table," Blackbeard instructed, "have fun!" He was the kind of teacher who didn't believe in too much control. He liked to give the children enough room to find their own way and, since he'd already explained the games in class, he chose not to recap. "You can put the music back on now Simon," he added.

"This table is for apple bobbing," said Thomas who, unlike his colleague, preferred to make sure things were being done properly. "One at a time. Katia - you go first."

Luke and Joe decided to come back later for apples and wandered over to see what was on the next table. Joe's treacle-covered scones, with long lengths of string tied to them, were suspended above the table and dangled at different heights. Queen Elizabeth I and Boudicca were already tucking in. With hands held behind their backs, Tania and Isabel tried to bite the scones and every time they got a nibble, the sticky pendulums swung away and then back, bumping their noses, their chins, their cheeks and their hair. Boudicca, being less concerned about her appearance than the Queen, finished her scone first and bowed her grinning, sticky head in gratitude for the applause of her peers. Queen Liz, dignified in defeat, shook her opponent's hand and went to the sink to wash her face.

"Us next!" said Luke, standing beside the table and leaning forward. "Go!" he shouted before Joe was ready, and tried to grab an untouched scone in his teeth.

Joe hurried to join in but found himself at

a disadvantage when one scone stuck to his thick beard, just below his bottom lip, and prevented him from getting close to any other. Thomas laughed and reminded Joe that he couldn't use his hands but he needn't have said anything because Joe was not a cheater. Luke was the clear victor, finishing his scone in just four bites, and afterwards Joe was allowed to manually detach his scone from his beard and eat it normally. There were less hairs on it than one might expect.

At the next table were small plates with chunks of barm brack on them, cut from the fruit breads that Luke and a couple of other people had made.

"I've got a coin!" said Isabel as she broke up her piece with a fork, "that means I'm going to be rich!"

"I think you're s'posed to just bite it," said Joe, "it might not work if you pull it apart like that."

"I don't wanna risk choking!" Isabel explained sensibly.

"Plus it's dirty," added Tania, "money's really dirty you know. Just think how many people have touched it without washing their hands."

Joe had already bitten into his chunk of barmbrack and discovered that he too had a coin. He spat it quickly into his hand.

"It's not dirty," Luke assured him, "don't ya think I washed 'em before I put 'em in?"

"Is this the one that you made?" Joe asked, a little relieved.

"Yeah," said Luke confidently, "well, it looks ..., yeah, definitely."

Luke bit into his piece of bread and found only currants and orange peel.

At the next table were three large dishes of colcannon, accompanied by a stack of small bowls and spoons. The game was the same. If you found a coin it meant you would be rich; if you found a ring it meant you would find true love. Luke hadn't had any rings to put into his baking, and he'd put all his spare coins into his barm brack, so he loaded his bowl from the colcannon he'd made himself, knowing that the only thing he was in danger of finding was a pile of delicious grub. Thoughtful as always, he didn't spoil the game for the others by telling them that.

A few minutes later, Luke, Joe, Tania and Isabel, all happy in spite of finding nothing but cabbage in their mash, found their newly stimulated appetites craved more and made their way to the long table. It was a good job they hadn't left it any longer as many of the other children were already digging in and the good stuff was going fast. Luke took a large paper plate from the pile and filled it with roasted sweetcorn, monkey nuts, roasted pumpkin seeds, bonfire toffee and ... oh no, Joe got the last toffee apple.

"Oh, do you want it?" Joe offered when his hand reached it just before Luke's.

"Nah," said Luke, trying to sound casual, "it's yours."

"We'll share it," Joe decided.

Luke smiled.

"Okay." This was a good party.

Then he noticed something bad on the table. Something not in keeping with the celebration. Something odious. Something which was in shockingly bad taste: scotch eggs.

"Hey! They can't have them on Halloween! Who brought them?" he asked, pointing with disgust at the flesh food and surveying the faces around the table.

"What's wrong?" asked Isabel.

Luke didn't hear her. He angrily snatched the plate from the buffet, intending to dispose of the offending items.

"Mr Beardsley said it's a Halloween tradition to be vegetarian," Joe explained to Isabel, "so Luke is cross that somebody's not doin' it right."

"So I see," said Isabel as she watched Luke trying to move through the crowd holding the large plate of scotch eggs above his head with both hands.

"Hey! Where you going with those?" Butler asked as Luke passed the music centre on his way to the toilets.

"Gettin' rid of 'em!" said Luke, "they're not Halloween."

"Hey! Bring them back! My mum made them! Bring them back!"

Luke hurried through the cloakroom door with Butler close behind him. The music stopped and everyone could hear the two boys arguing loudly on the other side of the door.

Luke Walker and the Halloween party

Mr Beardsley hurried after them.

"Don't come any nearer or I'll drop 'em," Luke threatened, forcing Butler to back off.

"You've got no right to throw away other people's stuff!" he shouted angrily, "you think you're better than everybody else! You think you're so good but you're not - you're a thief! Give them back!"

"It's no meat for Halloween!" Luke asserted, "dint your teacher tell you that?!"

"We don't have to do what you say! Some of us want to eat meat - most of us actually - coz it tastes good! Mmm, I'd love a nice bacon buttie right now, or a nice bit of fish and chips, or a big juicy burger."

His infuriating smirk pushed Luke to the limit and he lunged for the toilet door.

"Stop!" The boom of Mr Beardsley's voice did not encourage disobedience.

Luke froze, plate in hand, his back to his

teacher and his adversary.

"Could someone please tell me what on Earth is going on here?" Mr Beardsley asked more calmly.

Both boys talked at once: "He's throwing my mum's food in the toilet" / "Meat's not allowed on Halloween!"

"Stop!" their teacher said again, "Luke, what are you doing out here with that plate of scotch eggs?"

"They shouldn't be here! You said people dint eat meat on Halloween! It's tradition!"

"Yes, that's true, I did, it is traditional not to eat meat on All Hallows' Eve."

"But my mum made them! He's got no right to throw them away!"

"Simon!" Mr Beardsley quieted him, "no one's going to throw away your mother's food. Go back in to the party please and get the music going again."

Simon reluctantly did as he was told and Mr Beardsley turned back to Luke.

"Give me the plate please," he instructed.

"But they're not ..."

"Luke, now please."

Luke handed him the plate.

"But you're not gonna put 'em back on the table are you? They're not s'posed to be ..."

"Luke, I know you feel strongly about this and I respect that but you can't force your beliefs on other people. Everyone has to be free to make their own choices."

"Yeah right! Tell that to the chickens and pigs they're made out of! If they'd had free choice they would've said NO THANK YOU VERY MUCH, I DON'T WANT TO BE A SCOTCH EGG!"

"Yes, alright Luke you've made your point. Now kindly return to the party and stay away from Simon Butler."

Back in the classroom Luke found his plate

and his friends and told them the whole story.

"You're right," said Tania, "Simon knew he was supposed to make something from the traditional vegetarian recipes Mr Beardsley gave us. He should've been reprimanded for not doing it right."

"Typical!" added Isabel, "look at that, Beardsley's just putting the scotch eggs back on the table. That flies in the face of everything he taught us! What's the point of teaching us about historical tradition and saying you want to have a traditional party if you're just going to let people be inauthentic?"

"Yeah! It's fraudulent!" Tania concurred.

Luke hungrily polished off his sweetcorn while he listened to the impressive but unfamiliar vocabulary being employed by the girls and was in no doubt that they agreed with him.

"I think we should boycott this party!" Isabel declared.

Luke Walker and the Halloween party

"Whaddaya mean?" asked Joe.

"On the grounds that it's a sham."

"What?" said Luke and Joe at the same time.

"She means it's bogus," Tania explained, "spurious, phoney, false, fake."

"Oh, yeah, it's fake alright," said Luke, catching up, "he's ruined it. It's not thentick at all now!"

"If we want a truly educational, authentic, realistic, traditional Halloween experience, we'll have to do it ourselves," Isabel went on, "we should go now and play the other game he told us about. The one he said we couldn't play."

The others gasped and then grinned.

"That's ezzactly what we should do," said Luke.

***

A noisy, activity-filled party with only two adults in attendance was easy to sneak away from. It hadn't even been difficult to get the matches from Mr Beardsley's desk drawer. Fortunately there had been no rain for a couple of weeks so it didn't take long to find ample dry twigs and fir cones in the churchyard over the road. Now all they needed was a big stone each and that would be no problem either because Luke remembered seeing some different coloured pebbles, curiously arranged in the shape of a fish, close to the church entrance. They'd just been left there. No one was using them.

It was just after nine o'clock and very dark in the churchyard. Two owls hooted back and forth. Every so often bats flew overhead between the bell tower and the vicarage. Now it really felt like Halloween. The children made themselves comfortable on the ground near the oldest gravestones they could find. Covered in lichen, the writing on them was almost illegible.

Luke Walker and the Halloween party

Making sure there was nothing flammable nearby, Luke built a small fire with the twigs and fir cones on the crumbling horizontal stone base of one of the graves. He had no trouble getting it going with the few scraps of paper found in Mr Beardsley's desk drawer earlier.

As their teacher had told them, the game was simple. On Halloween night, participants made a fire and when the fire burnt out they placed a ring of stones in the ashes, one for each person. The following morning they would check the circle and if they found any stone displaced, it was said that the person it represented would die before the year ended.

Luke drew a circle in the ash with another stick. Their pebbles were easy to distinguish from each other. Luke's was the biggest and the darkest. He put it in the twelve o'clock position, closest to the gravestone. Joe's was a little smaller and had a notch on one side. He placed it at nine o'clock. Isabel's looked like it had a nose, hers was placed at six o'clock and Tania's, the smallest of them all, was placed at three o'clock.

"What was that?" Isabel turned suddenly to look behind her.

"Just a rabbit prob'ly," said Luke, "or a badger."

"Or a fox," added Joe.

The boys looked around eagerly, hoping to

see some majestic nocturnal wildlife. They weren't so lucky.

"We'd better get back," said Tania, looking at her watch, "it's nearly five to ten."

"Wait!" whispered Luke as he ducked behind a tree, "that's my dad!"

The churchyard was a short-cut between the school and Luke's road so he might have known his dad would come this way to meet him. Everyone laid low until he'd passed.

"My mum's probably at the school by now too," said Tania.

"They'll all be there, waiting outside the classroom for us," said Isabel anxiously, "how will we get back in without them seeing us?"

Luke and Joe smiled at each other. For seasoned outlaws like them, this wasn't going to be a problem.

"Follow us," said Joe, and they led the girls to a little known entrance to the school which was always left open when the caretaker was around so that he could duck out quickly for a smoke without going past the kitchens or the offices. The door led to the school hall which had a connecting door to Mrs Tebbut's classroom which shared a cloakroom with Class 5A.

"Don't tell anyone about this," Joe added as an afterthought.

Without raising suspicion all four of them rejoined the rest of their class as they emerged from the party. They parted with a secret promise to meet early Saturday morning and check on the fire circle. Each agreed to wait until they were all together before they looked.

When all children had been collected Mr Beardsley and Thomas returned to the classroom to clear up the mess. They were tired but it had been fun; they were glad they'd done it.

"Excuse me," Mrs Butler put her head round the door.

"Oh, hello," said Mr Beardsley, "are you looking for your plate? It's in a stack in the sink. I'll wash it up and send it home with Simon on Monday."

"Er, thank you, no, I'm looking for Simon. Did he leave with someone else?"

Mr Beardsley's jaw dropped. Filled with dread he looked at Thomas. Thomas shook his head. At that moment the classroom door opened again and Simon walked in.

"Simon! Where have you been?" his mum asked, awash with relief.

"Looking for you," he lied, "shall we go?"

Luke Walker and the Halloween party

Chapter Fifteen:

Luke Walker and the school play

Luke Walker and the school play

- "I am here today ..."

"Tonight."

- "I am here tonight to warn you, that you 'ave yet a chance and hope of escapin' my fate. A chance and hope of my procturin', Ebenezer."

"of my procuring."

- "Of my procurin' Ebenezer."
- "You were always a good friend to me, thank'ee!"
- "You will be haunted by three spirits."
- "Is that the chance and hope you mentioned, Jacob?"
- "It is."
- "I—I think I'd rather not."
- "Without the visits, you cannot hope to shun the path I tread. Expect the first tomorrow, when the bell tolls One."
- "Couldn't I take 'em all at once, and have it over, Jacob?"

"Don't move that, it's mine!"

"Luke! It's your line."

- "Expect the second on the next night ..

... hey! Leave it I said!"

"Luke!"

"That's my bag!"

"She's only putting it in the cloakroom, it's

Luke Walker and the school play

in the way out here, someone might trip over it."

"Oh."

"Can we please finish this scene! Go from 'Couldn't I take 'em all at once'."

Butler pulled a face at Luke who reciprocated.

- "Couldn't I take 'em all at once and have it over Jacob?"
- "Expect the second on the next night at the same hour. The third upon the next night when the last stroke of Twelve has ceased to vibrate. Look to see me no more; and look that, for your own sake, you remember what has passed between us!"

Ms Robinson breathed a sigh of relief.

"Okay, that'll do. Well done for getting the lines memorised both of you, but try to put a bit more feeling into it. Simon, remember you're really scared, and Luke, don't forget to rattle your chains and try to make your voice sound more ominous."

Simon laughed.

"I don't think Luke knows what ominous

means," he said with a smirk.

"Yes I do!" Luke replied indignantly.

Ms Robinson elaborated.

"Try to sound menacing, sinister. Make your voice deeper if you can."

"I knew what you meant!" Luke lied, flashing Butler his most withering scowl.

"Okay Luke, take a break," said Ms Robinson, "Simon, get in position for scene 3. First Spirit - where are you?"

Luke went to the cloakroom to find his bag. He didn't trust anyone else with it - there was important stuff inside. He was relieved to find it safe on his peg, looking as though it hadn't been tampered with. He confirmed this with the retrieval and measurement of his gobstopper - it was the same size it had been an hour and a half earlier when he'd put it in the zip pocket. He put the large sweet back into his mouth, took an orange plastic chair from the stack in the corner, and sat down to read his book. It wasn't really his book, he'd borrowed it from the library, but it was so good that he thought he'd get his own copy if he got any book tokens for Christmas. The funny thing was, if Mr Beardsley hadn't given them the book report assignment, he might never have picked it up. Its cover, a boring photograph of a corn field with a mountain behind it, would not normally have caught his attention, but its title - The Sustainability Secret - was intriguing. The word 'secret' had made him think of spies, secret agents, action and adventure, so he'd put the book on his 'maybe' pile and checked it out. He checked out seven books that day and after first trying and giving up on the other six, he decided, unequivocally, that The Sustainability Secret would be the subject of his book report. It turned out not to be about spies or secret

Luke Walker and the school play

agents but it was engrossing. He read it, and re-read it, every chance he got. Even when he was supposed to be watching rehearsals.

Participation in the school play had annoyingly failed to get him out of lessons because rehearsals were scheduled for after school and at weekends. On top of that Luke had had to spend an enormous amount of his free time learning his lines. Well, not an enormous amount, but some. As it turned out Luke was very good at memorising lines. Not only his own but those of everyone else in the scene. This was a very valuable skill to have and he determined to put it to more productive use in future. For example, there were lots of important facts in The Sustainability Secret that he wanted to commit to memory. A lot of it was scientific stuff which was harder to memorise but he wrote things down, over and over, until they stuck.

Luke Walker and the school play

After reading page ten he wrote in his secret society notebook:

"METHANE GAS FROM LIVESTOCK HAS A GLOBAL WARMING POTENTIAL **86** TIMES GREATER THAN CARBON DIOXIDE FROM VEHICLES"

After reading page eleven he wrote:

"FARMING ANIMALS FOR FOOD CONSUMES A THIRD OF ALL THE PLANET'S FRESH WATER, OCCUPIES UP TO **45%** OF THE EARTH'S LAND, IS RESPONSIBLE FOR UP TO **91%** OF AMAZON DESTRUCTION, AND IS THE LEADING CAUSE OF SPECIES EXTINCTION, OCEAN DEAD ZONES, AND HABITAT DESTRUCTION"

• "Good Heaven! I was bred in this place. I was a boy here!"

Butler's voice could really carry.

Finding it difficult to concentrate, Luke closed his book and put it away.

"If they've on'y jus' got to 'I was a boy here' it's gonna be ages 'til I'm on again."

He considered popping out to see Curly and Squirt but since time passed quicker when not at school he knew it was too risky. If he missed his cue again everyone would moan at him. He decided instead to hang out in the classroom. Pupils weren't really allowed in the classrooms without adult supervision, not since the "mindless vandalism" of class 6, but Luke felt that since he wasn't a mindless vandal, the rule didn't apply to him. The chairs were turned upside down on the desks; the bins were empty and the paint pots were washed up and stacked on the draining board. Everything except Mr Beardsley's desk was swept and dusted and tidy.

Mr Beardsley's desk was always a mess - he said it was the only way he knew where to find anything. Luke decided to see if there was anything worth finding. There were post-it notes, pencils, pens, two coffee mugs, a pencil sharpener, a stopwatch, a calculator - a calculator?!

"One rule for them, another rule for us!" thought Luke.

Luke Walker and the school play

There were two piles of exercise books - blue maths ones and yellow history ones. Luke sought out his own for a sneak preview of his grades.

"He hasn't even marked 'em yet!" he grumbled, exasperated, "what's the point of makin' us hand 'em in on Friday if you're not gonna mark 'em 'til next week?!"

There was nothing else of interest on top of the desk so Luke tried the drawer. It was unlocked.

"Aha!" He lifted out a large hardback diary, "let's see what you're gonna make us do next week."

He dropped the dog-eared book onto the desk and opened it to the first week of December.

Monday was left blank so Luke, cleverly imitating Mr Beardsley's handwriting, wrote:

watch a Christmas film

On the Tuesday page was a barely legible scribble which seemed promising:

Xmas Fish St. / / am

The Wednesday page foretold a spelling test and a fire drill.

The Thursday page confirmed what Luke already knew: there would be a full dress rehearsal of the Christmas concert in front of the rest of the school and the senior citizens from the village. He smiled, knowing that meant no lessons.

The Friday page contained a still more glorious statement:

End of term

•   "Yo ho there! Ebenezer!"

Luke flinched at Kenny's very loud portrayal of Fezziwig and knocked over one of the mugs which was still a quarter full of cold coffee. Thankfully, his reflexes were second to none and in slamming the diary shut he ensured the rest of the desk stayed more or less dry. He carefully placed the book back where he'd found it and rejoined his fellow Thespians.

***

"Will you check on Curly 'n' Squirt for me after school?" Luke asked Joe on Monday afternoon as the credits rolled at the end of Roald Dahl's *Matilda*.

"Yeah, why? Another rehearsal?"

"Yeah. I'll be glad when it's over an' done with."

"Not long now."

"Thank goodness!" said Luke with relief, "I think it was a mean trick them tellin' us we can be in the play without tellin' us we wunt be doin' the practices in lesson time."

"It was," Joe agreed, having had to give up a lot of his own free time to paint the scenery.

Luke Walker and the school play

Mr Beardsley switched on the lights and clapped his hands to get everyone's attention.

"Wakey wakey everybody, I hope you enjoyed that as much as I did. It's nearly half past three, so let me just remind you to bring your Christmas shopping money tomorrow. Full school uniform is compulsory - we don't want to lose anybody."

The bell rang loud and long, precipitating a riot of excited voices and chair legs scraping the floor.

"Exit quietly please," he requested, "see you tomorrow."

"I haven't got any money," said Joe to Luke confidentially.

"Me neither," Luke replied, "but that doesn't matter. It'll still be good to get out of school for a few hours."

Luke and Joe went their separate ways.

"See ya."

"See ya."

***

Luke made himself comfortable in the middle of the row of chairs at the back of the hall. He put his bag on the chair to his left, his coat on the chair to his right and his feet on the chair in front of him. He took out his reading book and his notebook, popped his gobstopper back in his mouth and, keeping one ear open for the approach of his cue, read.

- "Your reclamation, then. Take heed! Rise and walk with me!"

After reading page 71 he wrote:

FOR EVERY POUND OF SHRIMP THEY CATCH, THEY ACCIDENTALLY KILL TWENTY POUNDS OF OTHER MARINE ANIMALS.

After reading page 78 he wrote:

THE NUMBER OF BLUEFIN TUNA IS DOWN BY 96% BUT THEY ARE STILL LABELLED AS

SUSTAINABLY CAUGHT.

After re-reading page 69 he wrote:

THERE IS NO SUCH THING AS SUSTAINABLE FISHING. MARINE ENVIRONMENTS ARE IN TROUBLE. IF WE DON'T WAKE UP AND DO SOMETHING ABOUT IT, SCIENTISTS PREDICT WE WILL HAVE FISHLESS OCEANS BY 2048

- "Remove me! I cannot bear it!"
- "I told you these were the shadows of the things that have been. That they are what they are do not blame me!"

After reading page 80 he wrote:

OCEANS ARE THE CIRCULATORY SYSTEM OF THE PLANET. THEY PRODUCE OVER HALF THE WORLD'S OXYGEN AND ABSORB **70%** OF CARBON DIOXIDE. ALL LIFE ON EARTH DEPENDS ON THE HEALTH OF THE OCEANS AND THE HEALTH OF THE OCEANS IS DEPENDENT ON FISH AND THE INFINITE NUMBERS OF ECOSYSTEMS AT PLAY THERE.

IF THE OCEANS DIE, WE ALL DIE.

- "... but most of all beware this boy, for on his brow I see that written which is Doom, unless the writing be erased."

Luke swiftly returned his books and his gobstopper to his bag and hurried to stage left. It was time for the Third Spirit.

***

At ten forty-five on Tuesday morning, Luke

and Joe climbed aboard the school minibus and grabbed two of the back seats. Tania and Isabel grabbed the other two.

"This should be good," said Isabel.

"Yeah, I need to get something for my mum and something for my grandad," Tania replied.

"Is that all?" Isabel was impressed, "I've still got to do all mine."

The engine started.

"Okay everybody," Thomas shouted from the front, "seatbelts on. Off we go!"

Luke and Joe pulled their lunch boxes out of their bags. Isabel laughed.

"We'll be there in ten minutes," she said, "you shouldn't spoil your appetites - I bet there'll be some delicious Christmas food at the market."

"Nah, we'd rather eat now," said Luke as he bit into his blueberry muffin.

Tania looked over at their lunches and it reminded her of something she'd been meaning to

Luke Walker and the school play

tell them.

"Thomas is a veggie."

"Is he?" said Joe.

"I think so. I saw Mrs Tebbut offer him one of her homemade mince pies yesterday and he asked if they had vegetable suet in them. She said she wasn't sure so he said no thank you."

"He's cool," said Luke approvingly.

"Yeah," Joe agreed, "it's good he works in our class and dint stay with Ms Robinson."

***

The Christmas market was really crowded. It stretched the whole length of Fish Street which had been closed to traffic. Mr Beardsley told everyone to make sure they were always in sight of himself or Thomas. They were not to go off anywhere by themselves.

There was a Christmas tree at the car park end of the street, huge and covered in twinkling white lights. Next to it the Salvation Army band played Christmas carols and the whole atmosphere was happy and festive. The first stall sold reindeer food at a pound a bag, for anyone who wanted to leave a treat for Santa's friends on Christmas Eve.

At the second stall, if you weren't short of cash, you could buy a hand-calved Buddha.

The third stall looked more fun - they were selling robots playing snooker. Luke thought he wanted one but forgot about it as soon as he saw the bird whistles on the next stall. He'd always wanted to be able to communicate with birds.

The fifth stall sold snake-length marshmallows; the sixth sold Turkish Delight; the seventh had models of owls and elephants in jars; the eighth sold rock crystal lamps; the ninth had reindeer-shaped planters. Before long the market lost its charm for two boys with no money.

"Let's go over there," Luke suggested, pointing to an empty bandstand on the lawn behind the stalls.

"Mr Beardsley said we're s'posed to stay in sight," said Joe.

"We will be," Luke assured him, "we'll be able to see everybody from up there."

The boys squeezed between the chocolate scissors stall and the cannabis incense stall and climbed onto the raised platform of the bandstand. They sat comfortably with their feet dangling and tucked into their sandwiches while they watched the merry throng.

"This is good," said Luke smiling, "I don't mind shoppin' if I don't have to actually shop."

By the time they'd finished their lunches their classmates were out of sight and Joe felt they should try to catch up. Luke disagreed.

"No, we might get lost. We should wait coz they'll have to come back this way. Look, I can see the minibus from here."

"That's not our minibus. Ours doesn't have a green stripe down the side."

"Doesn't it?" said Luke, a little thrown. "Oh, well, they'll still have to come back this way. I think we should wait."

They only had to wait for another quarter of an hour before they saw a couple of familiar faces. Tania and Isabel were hurrying across the lawn towards them.

"There you are!" said Isabel, gasping for breath.

"Luke! - You've got to come! They're selling reindeer skins!" said Tania.

"And reindeer burgers!"

Luke and Joe, crestfallen, climbed down from the bandstand and followed the girls to the far end of Fish Street, where all the food

Luke Walker and the school play

stalls were. Luke was sad but not surprised to see what looked like hundreds of people eager to indulge in deep fried flesh foods, jostling to hold their positions in the queues.

"Say something!" Tania implored.

"What d'you want me to say?" Luke asked.

"Tell them they're despicable to kill reindeer! Tell them it's sick to sell reindeer burgers at Christmas!"

In addition to the stalls selling reindeer, there was one selling inferno cheddar (cheese laced with chillies); another was selling turkey sausages spiced with chilli and paprika; another was using a cute-looking model pig to sell pork scratchings.

"You can tell 'em that if you want," Luke said, loud enough to be heard by anyone who wanted to listen, "an' I agree with you, but it won't do any good. Not while there's so many stupid people who want to buy this stuff."

Luke Walker and the school play

"Who's stupid?" said a large man in the spicy sausage queue.

"You lot," said Luke unapologetically, "all you lot in these queues."

"Is that right?" he said slowly, turning to face Luke with eyes narrowed.

Tania and Isabel blushed and took a step back. Joe looked at his feet. Luke didn't move.

"Yeah," said Luke, "Don't you think it's stupid to pay for somethin' what's killin' the planet?"

A few more people turned to listen. Luke went on.

"Well, I call it stupid coz animal farmin' kills the sea and the rainforests and makes more greenhouse gases than cars an' planes an' all transport put together!"

"Says who?" asked the man sceptically.

"Said the United Nations. Over ten years ago." He paused briefly to let them absorb it before concluding. "Yeah, it's pretty stupid to spend your money on killin' the planet you live on. You're killin' yourselves. An' your children. An' your children's children."

Luke was surprised and disappointed to get almost no reaction to his shocking revelation, but he didn't give up. He had more.

"An' I should say it's pretty stupid to let people starve coz you paid for their food to be given to seventy billion farm animals, just so you can eat meat an' cheese. Yeah, anyone who pays for that is pretty stupid alright. And selfish."

The large man laughed stupidly.

"But it tastes so good!" he scoffed and turned back to wait for his sausage.

In the silence before the conversational hubbub rose again, three or four people walked away from the food stalls. Luke turned back to Tania and Isabel.

"See, there's no point tellin' people they're

horrible for sellin' horrible things. They don't care. They'll sell anythin' if people'll pay 'em for it. It's the people what pay for it who make it happen. If they didn't buy it, no one would sell it."

The girls nodded. Isabel looked guiltily at the half-eaten bag of pork scratchings in her hand and quickly tossed it in the bin. All four children walked back to the bandstand to look out for the rest of their class returning to the minibus. When they were back in their seats on the bus, Tania made a declaration.

"I'm going to make an early new year's resolution," she paused for effect before announcing, "I'm going vegan!"

"Me too," said Isabel, smiling.

Luke looked wonderingly at Joe. Joe nodded.

"D'you want to join our secret society?" they asked.

Luke Walker and the school play

Gingham County Primary School Presents

A Christmas Carol by Charles Dickens

Friday and Saturday evening at 7.30pm

Tickets
Adults: tickets £5.00. or £5.50 on the door
Concessions: tickets £3.00, or £3.50 on the door

Proceeds will go towards building a new classroom

- "Good Spirit, your nature intercedes for me, and pities me. Assure me that I yet may change these shadows you have shown me, by an altered life! I will honour Christmas in my heart, and try to keep it all the year. I will live in the Past, the Present, and the Future. The Spirits of all Three shall strive within me. I will not shut out the lessons that they teach. Oh, tell me I may sponge away the writing on this stone!"

Luke Walker and the school play

Chapter Sixteen:

Luke Walker and the

Maybury Christmas Fayre

Luke reached for it at the exact same time as Jared. They scowled at each other.

"Let me have it. I saw it first," Luke insisted.

"We saw it at the same time," Jared argued, "and I'm the oldest so you have to do what I say."

"I do not," said Luke emphatically.

"Boys!" Mr Walker halted their squabbling, "what's the trouble now?"

"I want to get this for Mum," explained Luke, "I saw it first."

"No he didn't!" argued his brother, "I saw it first and I want to get it for Mum."

The item in question was a dainty ceramic ornament depicting Little Bo Peep with a lamb - an ideal Christmas gift for anyone's mother. Dad took it off them and asked the lady how much it was.

"All the small ornaments are 50p," she told

him.

Dad looked at Jared and appealed to his better nature.

"Luke doesn't have much money Jared, so this is all he can afford. You've got your paper round money so you'll be able to find something else. Let your brother have this one."

Jared shrugged.

"Okay," he agreed and wandered off to the home-made jam stall.

Luke pulled a sticky fifty pence piece out of his pocket and handed it to the lady. She wrapped the ornament in tissue paper for him.

Dad smiled.

"Your mum'll love that Luke, nice find."

"Where is Mum?" Luke asked.

"Where d'you think?" said Dad, grinning.

"Tombola!" they both said at the same time.

This was the first time they'd been to the

Maybury Christmas Fayre and it was pretty good. There were lots of stalls where you could buy Christmas presents for reasonable prices - some things were second hand, some were home-made. There were games, like Mum's favourite, the Tombola, where you had to get a ticket ending in 5 or 0 to win a prize, and some which had a prize every time like the lucky dip or Luke's favourite where you paid 50p for a jar wrapped in Christmas paper without knowing what was in it. If you were lucky it might be a jar full of sweets or marbles; if you were unlucky it might be full of tea bags. But even that wasn't a complete loss because it could be a Christmas present for someone. Nan liked tea. There was also a cake stall, a raffle, and a dog show to see who was the prettiest dog and who was the cleverest dog and who was the most obedient dog. Luke knew that Dudley wouldn't enjoy that because he was the type of dog who had no interest in performing. He was clever, but didn't feel it necessary to prove that to anyone. He was his own dog and Luke respected that.

The other good thing about the Christmas Fayre was that it was in aid of helping animals. Maybury Centre for Animal Welfare was a sanctuary where they looked after horses and donkeys and sheep and chickens and tortoises and anyone else who needed help and came their way. They also rescued dogs and cats and rabbits and guinea pigs who'd been abandoned or neglected or cruelly treated, and they found happy new homes for them. Luke was very glad that his Christmas shopping money was going to such a good cause.

By three o'clock Luke had done all his shopping and was very happy with what he'd got for everyone: Little Bo-Peep for Mum; gloves for

Dad; football book for Jared; jar of tea for Nan; bowling DVD for Grandad; and a jar of marbles for Joe. Plus he'd been lucky enough to score a jar of gobstoppers and a really cool stainless steel whistle for himself.

Luke had 87p left so while Dad went to find Mum, he decided to have a final look round. In doing so he came across a man wearing climbing gear standing behind a table with a pen and a long list of names and numbers.

"Sponsor me to abseil down the clock tower?" he solicited.

"What's that?" asked Luke.

"Abseil means to descend down the side of a building on a rope."

Luke looked confused.

The man tried again to explain.

"So, I'll stand on the top of the tower wearing this harness attached to a rope which will be doubled through a loop. And I'll jump off the top and bounce my feet on the side of the tower, going down bit by bit, sliding the rope through my hands until I get the bottom."

"Yeah, I get what you mean, but why would you do that?"

"To raise money for Maybury."

"But why don't you get sponsored to do somethin' useful, instead of abstainin'."

"Abseiling," he corrected. "Raising money is useful for Maybury. They can do a lot of good things with it."

"Yes, but if the thing you got sponsored for doin' was useful as well, like you could get sponsored for pickin' up litter, then you would get money and at the same time you would have done somethin' really useful."

The man looked over Luke's head at the elderly couple approaching his table.

"Sponsor me to abseil down the clock tower?" he asked them.

Luke Walker and the Maybury Christmas Fayre

Luke moved on. When he got to the cafe he decided to pop in. He knew that 87p wouldn't ordinarily get him a cupcake but, since the end of the day was approaching, they might have made them half price. Or maybe there was a squashed one that nobody else wanted. It was worth a look. He stepped inside and picked up a menu. That was somewhat disturbing.

This animal sanctuary, this place of love and compassion, of respite and rescue; this place whose slogan, "We care about the well being of every animal", was written across every sign and above every doorway, was selling dead animals in its cafe.

Luke spoke to the lady behind the till.

"Why are you selling meat?"

"Erm, well, it's on the menu," she replied.

"But why is it on the menu?"

"Because it's a cafe," she said, not knowing why he was confused.

"It's a animal sanct'ry cafe," Luke pointed out, "and meat is dead animals."

"Ahh," she replied, finally understanding where he was coming from. "All of our meat is from local, free range farms."

"What does that mean?"

"It's sustainable."

"What does that mean?"

By this time a queue had formed behind Luke and when the manager saw that it wasn't moving, he came over.

"Is everything okay over here?" he asked the lady on the till.

"Oh, yes, erm, this young man has a question about the menu," she told him.

The manager steered Luke away from the counter.

"How can I help you?" he asked.

Luke started again.

"Why do you sell meat here?"

Luke Walker and the Maybury Christmas Fayre

"Because people want to eat it," the manager answered.

"But what about the animals who get killed for your meat?"

"Well, ..."

"And your eggs?"

"Ah, the eggs ..."

"And cheese and milk and ice cream?" Luke was getting louder and people were starting to look.

The manager spoke quietly in an effort to diffuse the situation.

"I assure you that all the meat, eggs, fish, and dairy sold here comes from local free range farms with sustainable practices."

Luke was exasperated.

"That's what she said!"

"Yes."

"What does that mean?"

"It means that it doesn't come from

factory farms where animals are kept in small cages. The animals are well looked after and are free to walk around."

"Until they're killed," said Luke.

"Er, yes," said the manager.

"And are the killin' sheds free range?"

"Er, no," the manager admitted.

"Are they special killin' sheds or are they the same killin' sheds what the factory farm animals go to?"

The manager knew a lot of eyes were on him and for a few moments he didn't say anything. Luke, however, had plenty more to say.

"They're the same horrible killin' sheds aren't they? And them animals is the same as the animals who you look after here; who you say you love; who you say should be treated kindly."

At this the manager felt he had a good come-back. He answered with confidence.

"Ah, no, we don't sell the meat of any of

the species who live at the sanctuary. Only beef and pork and fish."

Luke looked at him with disdain.

"And," the manager added with a smile, "we do have vegetarian and vegan options on the menu. We've got something for everyone."

Luke was bitterly disappointed in what he had thought was a wonderful place. That this was happening made absolutely no sense to him. He was so sick and tired of adults saying one thing and doing another. The manager, taking his silence as an end to their debate, turned to walk away. Luke touched his arm and said,

"So, you know about veggietareun food, you know there's no need to eat animals, but you still have 'em killed because some people like eatin' 'em. And Maybury says it wants to teach people how to be kind to animals but it doesn't set a good example of not eatin' 'em. It lets people think it's okay to eat 'em. It pretends it's not cruel to eat 'em so people keep on doin' it. So it's your fault when people keep on doin' it coz you could 'ave told 'em not to and you didn't."

He turned and walked out. He didn't want a cake any more.

"Luke! There you are!" called Mum, "you do have a penchant for wandering off."

Luke had no idea what a ponshon was but decided to take her word for it.

"Look what I've got!" she said. She sounded excited. "I won it! Well, I bought so many tickets I almost bought it!"

Luke looked at the slightly torn, slightly scratched, slightly coming apart at one end, box she was carrying. He could hardly believe it.

"Is that the same as ..?" he asked her.

"Exactly the same!" she said. She sounded so happy. "Here you are darling, this is yours." She was holding a Hornby R.793 King Size Electric

Luke Walker and the Maybury Christmas Fayre

train set. It was exactly the same as Grandad Pete's. Grandad Pete was Mum's dad and he loved trains. He was a volunteer fireman at his local steam railway and he used to let Luke ride the engine with him when they visited at Easter and August bank holiday. His Hornby train set had three locomotives - a King Henry VIII, a Class 29 (type 2) Bo-Bo, and a Class 3F Jinty Tank. Plus it had coaches, wagons, trackside accessories and buildings. It was brilliant.

Whenever they went to visit Grandad Pete, Luke and Grandad went up to the loft and played with the train set for hours. It was always set up. Always ready to play.

Grandad died the day after Luke's seventh birthday. He left Luke the train set in his will because he wanted it to go to someone who loved it as much as he had.

Sadly, Mum, because of an unfortunate series of events which were of no interest to Luke, accidentally backed over it with the car. Luke had been devastated. Mum equally so. She couldn't replace it because they didn't make them like that any more. And Luke didn't want just any train set. But now she'd found one. And it really was exactly the same as Grandad's. Luke was momentarily lost for words. He looked up at Mum's glowing face.

"Thank you," he tried to say but the words caught in his throat. He was overwhelmed.

"Can we go home and set it up?" he asked.

"Now?" she asked, "are we done here?"

"I'm done here," he replied.

***

Luke Walker and the Maybury Christmas Fayre

On Christmas Eve, Luke pulled down the peak of his blue engine driver's cap, blew his whistle and called,

"All aboard!"

The train pulled out of the station. It picked up speed and smoothly rode the tracks through Lego town, across the Scarf-River bridge, under the Bed-Tunnel through Bed-Mountain, and onto the Blue Pillowcase Coast. When it got to Seaside station it stopped to pick up Batman, Spiderman and a couple of soldiers on leave, before continuing on its journey to the end of the line. There was a near accident when a giant brown and white dog stepped onto the track but tragedy was averted when a quick-thinking observer lured the animal out of harm's way with a Digestive.

Outside, a car door slammed.

"Luke, Jared - Dad's home. He's got the tree!" Mum called from downstairs, "come down and help me decorate it."

Jared thundered down the stairs. Luke was too busy. Batman was late for a job interview - the train must keep going. As it sped towards the old suspension bridge, the driver noticed two of the shoe lace suspenders had snapped, and the others looked like they'd struggle to take the strain. He applied the brake but it was too late, the train was going too fast, it wouldn't be able to stop in time. Suddenly Spiderman climbed out of the window and ran along the roof of the train to the front. He spun his web and ....

Mum opened the bedroom door.

"Luke, don't you want to help decorate the tree?"

"erm, no thanks," he said without looking at her.

"Are you okay?"

"Yeah."

Luke Walker and the Maybury Christmas Fayre

"Are you sure? You haven't been yourself since we went to the Maybury Centre."

Luke didn't say anything. Mum tried again.

"What happened to upset you? I thought you'd like it there."

Luke let go of his trains, sat back and looked at her.

"I'm fed up."

"Why?"

"Coz I'm fed up of grown ups not doin' what they say."

Mrs Walker waited for more.

"Maybury is a animal sanctry wot says it teaches people to be kind to animals. A man from Maybury even came to give a talk at school to tell us not to keep animals in small cages, or let them have puppies."

"Okay,"

"So why do people whose whole job is lookin' after animals and teachin' other people to look after 'em prop'ly, still let animals be killed for food? Why don't they care about them animals? Why do they on'y care about some animals?"

"What makes you think ..."

"They sell dead animals in their cafe."

"Really? That does surprise me."

"If I can't trust people whose job is lookin' after animals then I can't trust nobody. 'cept myself!"

"Ooh, that's hard. No wonder you're fed up," said Mum sympathetically.

"And Joe," he admitted.

"Well, that's something. But you know Luke, you shouldn't give up. You should tell them how you feel. You should tell them you are offended by their decision to sell meat in their cafe."

"I did tell 'em."

"Good. And what did they say?"

"Nothin' sensible. Jus' said it was okay coz

it was rangin' and stainable. Rubbish!"

"Tell them again. Write them a letter."

"What's the point? They won't take no notice o' me."

Mrs Walker was sorry her son felt so discouraged. It was a terrible thing to lose your faith in humanity at such a young age.

"The thing is," she told him, "you never know when someone might listen. The only thing you can be sure of is that if you don't say anything, they definitely won't get the message."

Luke looked at her and didn't say anything.

"Come with me, come and help decorate the tree," she said.

When they got to the living room Jared and Dad already had things well underway. The tree was gleaming with glittery gold and silver tinsel and different coloured shiny baubles.

"Mm, pretty good," said Mum, "but it's missing something."

"The star for the top," said Jared, "I'm just about to do it."

"Something else," said Mum and she left the room.

A moment later she was back with a small box from the kitchen. She handed it to Luke.

"No Christmas tree is complete without a few sweet treats," she said, smiling.

Luke looked in the box. It was full of chocolate Santas. On the wrappers were the words:

Moo Free Organic Chocolate,
DAIRY FREE, GLUTEN FREE, VEGAN

Luke's jaw dropped and his eyes lit up.

"Are these for me?" he asked.

"No, greedy boy, they're for all of us! Why don't you hang them on the tree?"

"But, ... how come ...?"

"I found your leaflets," Mum explained.

"What leaflets?"

Luke Walker and the Maybury Christmas Fayre

"The ones stuffed in the back pocket of your black cords; the black cords you shoved under the bed and forgot about I don't know how long ago."

"Oh, I wondered where they were."

"Well I found them and I checked the pockets before putting them in the wash, and there were these leaflets. One with a picture of a cow on the front entitled 'The Dark Side of Dairy' and one with a cute little brown and white piglet on the front entitled 'Think Before You Eat'."

"And you read them?"

"And I read them."

"And that's why ...?"

"Yes it is," she paused for a moment, searching for the right words. "Luke," she went on, "you have good instincts. When you started this crusade for animals you did it on instinct. You hadn't been told any of the shocking facts and figures that are in those leaflets, you just knew it wasn't right. And you did something about it. You spoke out bravely and you acted. You broke the rules when you felt you had to and you endured punishments, but you never wavered; you never stopped fighting."

Luke nodded. He wasn't sure why his mum was explaining something that she must have known he already knew, but he waited. It would become clear eventually. She continued.

"So I don't want you to give up hope now. I want you to know that if you keep trying, you will make a difference. You have already made a difference for Curly and Little Squirt and the rabb..., er, the damsons, but even more than that, you're a good influence on other people."

Now, those were words Luke never thought he'd hear from his mother.

"You have been a good influence on us."

At this point she took his hand, led him

Luke Walker and the Maybury Christmas Fayre

into the kitchen and opened the freezer.

"What d'you fancy for Christmas dinner?" she asked.

Luke looked in the freezer. It was full - Mum always did a big shop for the Christmas holidays - and there were quite a few unfamiliar boxes and cartons. He lifted them out one at a time to read the descriptions:

Cauldron Wholefood Burgers
Made with Chickpeas, Cauliflower, Aduki Beans, Broad Beans, Spinach, Onions, Garlic & Potatoes
Cauldron Wholefood Sausages
Made with Grilled Vegetables (Peppers, Cougette, Onion), Beans & Wheat
Cauldron Aduki Bean Melt
"The combination of aduki beans, spinach and mushrooms deliciously filled with mango chutney and carefully coated in breadcrumbs gives a satisfyingly moreish taste."
Biona Red Lentil Sun Seed Burger
A flavoursome vegan burger made with red lentils, pumpkin and sunflower seeds with a subtle hint of spice. Made using all natural, organic ingredients and free from artificial colours or flavours. Perfect loaded with your favourite burger toppings, added to salads or dipped in sweet chilli sauce as a tasty and nutritious snack.
Can be eaten hot or cold.
Dee's 6 Leek & Onion Vegan Sausages
The perfect partner to velvety mashed potatoes and homemade gravy, our Leek and Onion Sausages will become an instant family favourite on your weekly menu.

Dragonfly Organic Bubble & Squeak Tatty

Our Tatty is a vegetarian burger that has a real bubble & squeak feel about it, made using locally sourced cabbage and onions

Linda McCartney Vegetarian Country Pies

Vegetarian pie made from a shortcrust pastry base, filled with rehydrated textured soya protein in a rich onion and beef-style gravy, topped with a puff pastry lid.

Linda McCartney Vegetarian Sausage Rolls

Vegetarian Cumberland sausage-style filling wrapped in puff pastry.

And there were three flavours of luxury organic vegan ice cream:

Booja Booja Hazelnut Chocolate Truffle, **Booja Booja** Raspberry Ripple and **Booja Booja** Caramel Pecan Praline.

Luke was no longer fed up. He smiled broadly at his mum.

"Are these for all of us?"

"Yes they are. For all of us," she said happily, "and I got them from Besco's. They sell them in mainstream supermarkets Luke and that just shows how much progress you're making. That's what happens when you speak out and you keep speaking out."

Mrs Walker was treated to a rare hug which lasted a good half minute, and then Luke ran from the kitchen.

"Where are you going?" she called after him.

"I've got some letters to write!" he said.

Luke Walker and the Maybury Christmas Fayre

Also by Violet Plum

* ### Luke Walker: animal stick up for-er
  (The first eight chapters)
  ISBN: 978-1530509638

* ### Luke Walker: animal stick up for-er: my privut notebook
  (a must-have for all members of Luke's
  Secret Society of animal stick for-ers)
  ISBN-13: 978-1530311286

* ### Big Blue Sky (A Christmas Story)
  (A colourfully illustrated moving story, told
  from the point of view of two turkey brothers
  who dream of seeing the sky. It ends happily
  and magically on Christmas Eve.)
  ISBN-13: 978-1539784739

* ### The Princess Who Liked To Be Popular
  (A traditional-style fairy tale with modern
  relevance about a princess who tries too hard
  to please everyone, with dire consequences!)
  ISBN-13: 978-1505669572

Find these and many other titles at
Little Chicken Books
little-chicken.net

Made in the USA
Columbia, SC
04 December 2017